To a man with hwyl

COMING ALIVE

Judith Cutler

ISIS

LARGE PRINT

Oxford

Copyright © Judith Cutler, 2000

First published in Great Britain 2000
by Severn House Publishers Ltd.

Published in Large Print 2003 by ISIS Publishing Ltd,
7 Centremead, Osney Mead, Oxford OX2 0ES
by arrangement with
Severn House Publishers Ltd.

British Library Cataloguing in Publication Data
Cutler, Judith
    Coming alive. – Large print ed.
    1. Widows – Great Britain – Fiction
    2. Large type books
    I. Title
    823.9'14 [F]

ISBN 0–7531–6983–5 (hb)
ISBN 0–7531–6984–3 (pb)

Printed and bound by Antony Rowe, Chippenham

CHAPTER
ONE

The sea mist was snaking up the quiet Devon valley and thickening the darkness.

Even the solitary streetlight gave no more than the palest of glows. Behind its straggling hedge, its sagging gate, the cottage seemed further away from her home than ever. It was very cold.

Bracing herself, Rebecca twitched the curtains closed. No, she mustn't allow herself to give way. Of course she was miserable. But she must just get stuck in, and make the best of it.

The problem was knowing just where to start.

Owen Griffiths reversed the Volvo round to the front of Penkridge House. Tim was waiting for him, grinning as his father negotiated the tight bend in the drive. Owen grinned back through the back window. But he wondered just how much longer he could enjoy the sunny company of his only son. Although Tim was fourteen, he'd never yet behaved as if he was in the turbulent rapids of the teens. But any moment now Tim might rebel against the routine that Owen's busy life imposed on them both. In theory Tim was a week-day boarder at Low Ash school, coming home every weekend. In reality he spent more and more weekends confined in school. It might be known for its good exam results, but Owen was beginning to have doubts about other aspects of the school. Stronger doubts: he'd never been quite happy with the place. One of these days he and Tim would have to have a proper talk about it.

The trouble was, Tim wasn't one to complain — he'd been the easiest, sunniest of babies, smiling happily at a succession of nannies. Not so many, in fact. Owen — and Tim — had always been fortunate. The women who'd come to live with them in this quiet corner of Devon had almost all been kindly and reliable. There'd only been that one devastating evening when Tim, playing in the bath, had turned to Owen and asked, "Next time I have a nanny, can I have one that loves me?"

At that moment, if Owen could have laid hands on Helena, the wife who'd left him with a three-week-old baby to concentrate — as she'd put it — on her career, he would have killed her. Career! That might have been some excuse, if not a reason. But her idea of a career had been simply to move on to another man, one much richer and with better opportunities than she thought Owen would ever have. And then another man. And another. Owen's constant dread was that she would come sneaking back into their lives. Oh, not for love. She'd never shown the slightest interest in Tim, except to send Christmas and birthday gifts. But because she now knew Owen was a better prospect than she'd realised.

2

"Let's get this lot aboard!" Owen called, getting out of the car and pointing to the things Tim considered essential for a bearable life at Low Ash. "What have I done to deserve a son who plays not just the cello but the bass guitar?"

Tim hefted the guitar case. "Could have been worse, Dad. I could have chosen the drums and the double bass."

"And it could have been the piccolo and the triangle! OK. What about your school bag? You've spent all those hours sweating over that assignment — it'd be a shame to forget it."

Tim dashed off, his blond thatch gleaming under the porchlight. Owen shivered. The boy was so young, so vulnerable. He'd have given everything to be able to give his son the settled home life he deserved. Everything except his work. After years of unrewarding slog, Owen was now being offered the film scores he wanted. And that meant travel, long hours of work, and being there when others wanted him.

Tim was back. "Where are you off to this week, Dad?" he asked, slinging his school bag into the back of the car.

Owen pretended to yawn with boredom. "Hollywood, I'm afraid." But he put his arm round Tim's shoulder and they laughed together. "And you may have to spend next weekend at Low Ash, I'm afraid."

Tim shrugged. "Well, there'll be the auditions for the Christmas play. And there'll be a rugger match for us all to go and cheer at." This was the nearest Tim ever got to complaining: a bit of irony about sport.

Owen tried to pick up his son's mood. "Well, that *will* be exciting, won't it? Any idea what play they've got in mind?"

Tim pulled a face. "Old man Cowley's got this idea that it would be exciting to put on all-male Shakespeare. Without Gwyneth Paltrow. And the word on the street is it's *Hamlet*. Without Mel Gibson."

"Or even Branagh? Tut, tut. So who do you think will play Hamlet?"

Tim snorted. "Got to be Tony, hasn't it? I mean, no one else could manage it. Curtis would like to think he could, but he can't hold a candle to Tony." He slipped into the passenger seat, fastening his seatbelt as his father locked the house.

Owen hurried back to the car. "What will you audition for?" He leaned forward to fit the key in the ignition. Not for Ophelia, please God. The last thing Owen wanted was for his quiet, gentle son to be thrown too much into the company of a glamorous older boy. Although Tony, the headmaster's son, practically lived here at weekends, he still felt he knew very little about him. The rumour was that Tony had been thrown out of another, more prestigious school, for taking drugs. Worse — for Owen was a realist — for dealing them.

Tim waited until the engine had fired. "Sounds as if this is due for a service, Dad. I rather thought of Osric, actually. It wouldn't be too much to learn and it could be quite funny."

Owen hoped his sigh of relief wasn't too audible.

"Trouble is, Cowley's got his own ideas about casting. And I've got this nasty suspicion that he won't

4

find one of us to take on Gertrude, and Ma Cowley will end up playing her. Poor old Hamlet, having her slobbering all over him! Yuck!" he shuddered.

Owen couldn't argue. Cowley had been producing the school play since the year dot, apparently, and made a habit of casting his eternally unsuitable wife as the mature lead. If Hamlet was a schoolboy, she'd be old enough to be his grandmother — she'd retired from her post as librarian in the summer.

He picked his way cautiously down the drive. The fee for this film should help him pay for some urgently needed resurfacing. Maybe some lights at regular intervals — much needed on a murky night like tonight. He hated Tim coming and going in complete darkness either on foot or on his bike. OK, so Devon wasn't an inner-city slum, where muggers or murderers might be hiding behind every bush, but it wasn't paradise either. There were rumours of a peeping Tom, and one woman claimed to have been tailed for miles through the narrow lanes to her house, where only the presence of her husband and a large Alsatian had deterred her stalker.

God! Did all parents worry like this? And did they all have the same struggle not to let their child see their fears?

He made an effort. The last thing he wanted was for Tim to start worrying about why he was so silent. "So who have they found that's mug enough to live in that place?" he asked, pointing at a cottage just outside the school gates. A light was visible through a slit in the curtain.

"Dunno. But they must have needed a machete to cut their way to the front door." Tim shifted in his seat.

"What's the matter?"

"Just sitting to attention. After all, we have just entered the hallowed grounds of Low Ash School."

CHAPTER
TWO

Tim lay still, listening to the noises penetrating the flimsy cubicle walls. Someone was grinding his teeth, someone else muttering in his sleep. No one was crying today, at least. He sighed with relief. Since Tony had sailed into the school, halfway through the last summer term, there'd been much less bullying. As Tim had reason to know. Not that anyone had ever picked on him particularly. Not when they'd realised how fast a bowler he was. Not when they'd realised that a bass guitarist like him would hold the school group together. Until then there'd been a couple of tricky moments. Trouble was, he wasn't big or heavy enough to defend other minnows. Tony was both: swift to react with either a withering tongue or a vicious punch, if that were ever needed. Hero he wasn't, though. Tim realised that, even if the others didn't. No, Tony might be eighteen, nearly six foot tall and lording it in the Upper Sixth, but he was as troubled as anyone in the school.

But even Tim didn't dare to try and find out the cause of the problem. Tony's father apart, that is. Mr Clifford-Payne. Who from day one was obviously going to be Payne-in-the-Arse. And he wasn't the headmaster but the Chief Master, with not a house but a Lodging in the grounds. Tim suspected that his father had a very good idea what a pompous idiot the man was, though they'd never discussed it. And just because you could laugh at him behind his back didn't mean he couldn't be quite scary if he wanted to. Which was quite often, although there were some days he seemed almost human. He'd certainly been good about allowing Tim extra time for his music, even if it had been quite plain he'd have preferred him to be practising the cello rather than the guitar. And as it happened — though Tim made sure no one in the school, master or pupil, knew it — it was the cello he preferred. His father's son, he supposed. But he enjoyed the guitar, and not just because it brought him respect from the other boys.

Although the rising bell hadn't sounded, Tim got up. He could put in at least half an hour on that Bach piece if he got moving now. And, he reflected, as he headed for the lavatories and the showers, the place was a lot more civilised when you could have a bit of privacy.

It had probably taken only five minutes for the word to whiz round the school that there was a new woman in the building. The information included the fact that she wasn't young and hadn't any tits worth mentioning. The tone in which the news was relayed left it in no doubt that it was every boy's duty to make her life as miserable as possible without actually giving her an excuse to complain to Clifford-Payne. Tim had a nasty feeling that any tormenting wouldn't be confined to the boys, either.

"Sure, the Swine'll have a go at her," Tony agreed, falling into step with Tim outside the library. "Loathes women. Look at the way he used to speak to Ma Cowley. He'd have enjoyed burning witches."

"Except he'd soon have run out of witches."

"Not as long as there was a woman left in the village!"

"What's she going to be doing here, anyway?" Tim asked. After all, if anyone got inside information, it ought to be Tony.

"Poor cow, I've a nasty suspicion the OB may be lining her up as a replacement for Mum."

OB. Old Bastard. At least he didn't think of Owen like that. "What's she like, then?" Tim asked cautiously.

Tony shrugged. "Never met her. But I think I'm about to. Look, there she is. The Old Bastard's only made her librarian!"

The boys stopped just outside the door, surveying her.

"She doesn't look much like a wicked stepmother," Tim said at last.

Nor did she. She was slender to the point of thin, dressed like a refugee from a jumble sale, and had badly cut mousy hair.

"Doesn't look much like a stepmother at all," Tony conceded. "How old d'you reckon she is?"

Tim had only just got beyond the point when he thought everyone who wasn't clearly young must be old. He paused: perhaps Tony would think he was going to make a sophisticated and informed guess. "Thirty-ish? Forty-ish? Hard to tell with those clothes. And no make-up, of course."

Tony stared, in mock amazement.

"Well, she's not like Dad's friends' women," Tim said. "Or any of the potential stepmothers Dad's brought home for me to inspect. Not that his heart was in it, mind. So I didn't encourage him."

"I don't think I can encourage the OB to marry *her*. Much too young for him, the old ram."

"Too young?"

"Well, I wouldn't put her above thirty-five. Oh, God. Come on, kid. Time the Fifth Cavalry rode to the rescue. Friend Curtis is exercising his charms on her!"

Curtis, Captain of Rugby, was renowned for his strength and power on the pitch and his cruelty off it. Whatever Tony had had to say or do to get him off Tim's back, Tim had never yet discovered. All he knew was that since Tony's arrival he felt as if the air was his to breathe again. No more assaults, verbal or physical. No more sexual remarks that he never knew were jokes or propositions.

Curtis had readily assumed that Tim and Tony were more than friends, and had almost certainly been responsible for pushing the rumour about the school. Tony had heard about it first, and had made a point of coming to see Tim up at Penkridge House at a time when he knew Owen would be around. Tim didn't know what he'd told Owen, but his father seemed reasonably happy with the conversation. Not that Owen seemed to like Tony much more — he still regarded him, with his drugs history, as someone best kept at a distance.

Tony slouched into the library, Tim at his heels. Curtis was leaning on a large table.

"Hey," Tim whispered, pointing to it, "where did she get hold of that?"

"Looks as if she means business. Let's help her get on with it."

The new librarian had placed the table between herself and the rest of the room. She was clearly trying to make some sense of the filing and issues system, with cards spread everywhere. And Curtis, with one strong index finger, was quietly and obviously disarranging them as he spoke to her. Whatever he was saying was drawing a blush so deep that Tim almost winced at her pain and embarrassment.

"You're taking a risk, aren't you, Curtis? Hanging around here when Dad's looking for you? Sorry to interrupt," Tony smiled at the woman. "But you know what my dear father's like when he's kept waiting."

Curtis peeled himself off the desk and shoved his hands ostentatiously deeply into his pockets, where he proceeded to play with coins or keys. Possibly.

Tony stared at him, one eyebrow raised. "Bit old for pocket billiards, aren't you?"

Curtis shrugged and left. Tim had been practising the same cold and arrogant movement but, as his efforts before the bathroom mirror showed, without much success.

Tony's face returned to normal as he spoke, so quietly that even Tim hardly heard. "He's a yob. A nasty, predatory yob. Tell him where to get off," Tony looked at her wedding ring, "Mrs — er — ?"

"Wildbore. Rebecca Wildbore." She almost put out a hand to be shaken, but must have realised that that wasn't how to greet mere pupils, so she withdrew it, flushing again.

But Tony shoved his forward. "Nice to meet you. And welcome to Low Ash. I'm Tony Payne. The Chief Master's son. And this is my friend Tim Griffiths."

Tim found himself shaking hands, too. "Thing is, Mrs Wildbore," he said, "there's one or two people — you know, they'll try to take advantage of you. Being new, you know. So if there's anything you need to know — about anything or anyone — you just ask Tony or me."

"One of the things you need to know is that there's a silence rule in here," Tony said, very quietly. "And Mr Swain over there — we know him as the Swine — is just coming to tell us off for breaking it. You just point us in the direction of those books over there and maybe we'll all get away with it." And he grabbed Tim by the shoulder before Mrs Wildbore had time to reply.

Though they escaped a bollocking, it was clear she wouldn't. Even from where they stood, they could see her blushing again, and Tim had a nasty feeling she wiped her eyes when Swain had finished with her.

CHAPTER
THREE

Rebecca Wildbore had presented herself outside Clifford's study at eight thirty in the morning. His secretary had pointed a bored finger in the approximate direction and returned to her computer. Rebecca had to admit she couldn't have missed the door.

The Chief Master
Mr D.L. Clifford-Payne, MA (Cantab), M.Ed.
Knock and wait

She knocked. And waited. At last — just as she was wondering if the room were empty — a peremptory voice demanded, "Come!"

She entered to find him smoothing down his gown.

"Clifford —" she began, with an eager smile.

She didn't like his expression.

"My dear Mrs Wildbore," he said, "I do really think that, given the formality of our circumstances, you should address me by my full name. A better example for the boys. Or, if you prefer, you could use the term, 'Chief Master'. So much more professional, don't you think?"

She could do no more than nod.

"Now, I've asked our senior English master to show you the library. He should be here at any moment." He sat down and flicked through some papers.

She waited, looking around her. The room was dark, heavily panelled and decorated with portraits of long-dead bewhiskered clerics. They looked like former headmasters. As far as she knew, however, the school had opened only in the seventies. Clifford's predecessor had bought the Victorian house when it was sold to pay off death duties.

At long last, he looked up and blinked, as if surprised she was still there. "I trust your accommodation is comfortable."

She made an effort. "There are — one or two problems, Chief Master."

"Bring them to the attention of the bursar, if you please." There was a knock at the door. "Come!" he called immediately. "Ah! Cavendish!"

Cavendish was a tall and broad-shouldered man of about her own age. He nodded curiously at her, but addressed himself to Clifford. "Good match on Saturday, Sir. And even the under-fifteens acquitted themselves reasonably well."

Clifford nodded. "Curtis is coming on very nicely, isn't he? I have an idea we may be seeing him at representative level before too long. The county at least."

"Thompson, too. He's got a good turn of speed these days. And if he can put on a bit more weight — build up his muscles . . ." He stopped.

"I'll have a word with Matron," Clifford said crisply. "Now, Jeremy, if I might trespass on your time, perhaps you'd direct Mrs Wildbore here to the library. Show her the ropes."

"What few ropes there are, Chief Master."

Clifford didn't respond. Perhaps he did not find that sort of quip amusing. Instead, he flicked a glance at his watch.

Cavendish took the hint. "We'll be on our way, then, Sir." He turned and opened the door.

Rebecca risked a brief smile over her shoulder at Clifford, but he was already bent over his papers. She followed Cavendish as he and his billowing gown swept out, like a rowing boat in the wake of a clipper.

Gown? What school expected its teachers to wear gowns? There'd been a story in one of the papers about teachers no longer being allowed to wear jeans. No one had expected them to don gowns! But he set such a rattling pace through the corridors she couldn't ask any questions about anything. She couldn't even register their route. How on earth would she find her way back? At last, they paused long enough for Cavendish to fish for keys and push open a set of double doors.

So this was the library! She looked askance at her new kingdom. Where would she start? Cleaning the three-quarters empty shelves or trying to re-fill them from the piles of books stacked behind the sort of desk they'd used at university for exams?

"Old Ma Cowley didn't have much idea, did she?" Cavendish remarked.

"She didn't have much space to operate from," she retorted. "Now, I shall need a proper table. We'll move that one from there for the time being."

Shrugging, he helped her.

"Thanks. And now could you show me where everything else is?"

"Everything else?"

"Date stamps, cards, things like that," she said, surprising herself with her crisp reply. "I assume you're not computerised."

Cavendish looked taken aback. Was it because she was making demands or because she was asking stupid questions? "Hardly. Not in a place this size. After all, there's no likelihood that the boys will run away with the books, is there?"

She looked at the shelves. "Someone has."

"Oh, that's one of the things you'll have to do. Trawl through the desks and lockers — see what you can find."

"Do you mean — when the boys aren't there?"

"Why not?" he asked carelessly, pulling a copy of the *Western Morning News* towards him.

"Because — because — that would be . . . an invasion of their privacy. Surely Clifford — Mr Clifford-Payne — could make an announcement at assembly telling the boys to return books for checking?"

"That wasn't what he said." He turned the paper to read the back page.

"But —"

16

"You don't like it, lady," Cavendish said, like the star of a B movie, "you tell him. OK?" He picked up the paper. "Anything else?"

She looked helplessly around. "Dusters?"

"Bursar." He headed for the door.

"Keys!"

"Keys?"

"To lock and unlock these doors."

He shrugged. "Bursar. In the meantime, you'll have to find a master to do it for you. Send one of the lads."

"And if a master is unavailable?" But she knew the answer already.

"You'll just have to wait, won't you?"

Clifford-Payne; Cavendish; Curtis. And then the encounter with Swain those boys had predicted.

"You are obviously unaware, my good woman, of the need for silence in a library." He looked her up and down, his eyes reptile-cold. Once his hair must have been red with the white skin that goes with it. The hair might have turned rusty, but his face was still startlingly pale. "Quite why the Chief Master should appoint someone without librarianship qualifications is beyond me. It is, however, a part-time and thus a temporary appointment, so I am quite sure you will have the motivation to learn."

Even as her eyes filled — she'd thought only Rupert spoke to people like that — anger flared. How dared Clifford tell his staff she was unqualified? Undercutting her before she'd even started the job? And from what she could gather, even if her predecessor had been an expert in her field, she'd certainly been slipshod in the way she'd carried out her everyday work.

She'd spent the rest of her stint trying to sort the pile of books into some sort of order. No one seemed to have thought of using the Dewey or any other system of classification. The shelves themselves had tattered labels attached to them with yellowing sticky tape: ENGLISH; LANGUAGES; SCIENCES. After her lunch-break, she'd find the bursar, and get hold of some dusters. At least the books and shelves would be cleaner by the time she'd finished.

She looked at her watch. She should have left the library ten minutes ago. It seemed to her quite crazy to close a library at precisely the time she'd have expected it to be busy, but that was what her schedule said. She looked down the library corridor yet again. There was no sign of anyone, boys or masters. The obvious thing, to stay as long as she had to and return proportionately later. But she was sure that this would enrage Clifford. He would expect her to keep to the hours he'd laid down, and whatever the reason for a late return he would condemn her. Probably publicly.

So she was stuck. She was desperately thirsty and equally in need of a lavatory. And hungry, too. Unpleasant though the smell of the boys' dinner might be — did schoolboys still have to eat overcooked cabbage? — it made her mouth water.

She had never felt so helplessly alone.

At last, swift footsteps! Someone was breaking the no-running rule.

Tony!

"I thought so!" His grin was angry. "I thought they'd leave you here. Come on. Time you pushed off."

"No key," she said.

"What do you think this is?" He flourished it. "The master key. My esteemed parent has this habit of leaving his keys lying on his dressing table. The obvious thing was to get a copy. Here. You have it."

"Aren't I supposed to see the bursar?" No, she didn't sound plaintive: she sounded sarcastic.

He grinned. "And what's the betting he won't be able to lay his hands on a spare? In any case, Monday's his day for doing the accounts. No one is allowed to interrupt."

"But —"

"Just take it, Rebecca," he said, unclipping it from his ring. "Just take it. And shift — what's the betting my esteemed parent will just happen to come this way to check if you're back here on time?"

The smell of damp oozed over her as she opened the cottage door. How could Clifford have encouraged her to think she would have decent accommodation? This! No, he couldn't have seen it. He must have taken someone's word for it — the bursar's, perhaps! Taking a last gasp of fresh air, she pushed through the living-room into the kitchen. And wished she hadn't. The mould . . .

It was either cry or push her shoulders back and use that bleach she'd found amidst the rubbish in the decaying outhouse. One day she must buy a bigger lightbulb, too. This was so dim she might as well be using candles.

She grabbed the remains of the loaf Margaret, her sister-in-law, had left her, and some of the cheese. A glance at the enormous clock — why had anyone installed such a loudly ticking monstrosity in such a tiny space? — told her she had no time for the refinements of a sandwich. Cheese in one hand, bread in the other, she grabbed some of her own dusters and set off back up to the school. By now it was raining hard enough to soak the bread into an unappetising mush. Better get it down quickly, then.

But she was still hungry. She thought that over the years she'd have trained herself not to notice hunger pangs. Her only source of cheap food had been her garden. When Rupert had declared he was too busy to look after it, she'd managed to grow a few vegetables herself. Carrots, celery. Quick munches. If only she could rely on the garden here. There was certainly room for a good crop — if only she could clear the ground. It was full of docks and goodness knows what else. Somewhere at the far end was a tangle of blackberries, but they were mildewed, of course, so late in the year and with all this rain. Glorious Devon! Someone had never seen it like this!

If only she weren't so hungry . . .

Someone's windfalls lay uncollected in the lane. Like a thief, she bent to pick up a couple. Yes. They were sound enough. Rubbing them on her sleeve, she bit in.

They were the sweetest things she'd come across since she'd arrived.

As she walked briskly up the long drive to the school buildings, she had to move over to make way for a car. Clifford's big Saab. It stopped. The window rolled down.

"My dear Mrs Wildbore, can I really believe my eyes? That like some country bumpkin you're walking in the school grounds eating an apple? For goodness' sake, what sort of example are you setting to the boys?"

Before she could reply, the window closed and the car pulled away. From somewhere sprang an awful urge to stick her tongue out at it. She might almost excuse him for the rebuke — if it were really true that eating in the grounds was forbidden. But not to offer her a lift, in this weather! If only she could tell him where to put his miserable cottage, his miserable job and his miserable manners!

Clifford's behaviour had been altogether very strange today. She'd known him for years: he and Rupert had been close enough friends for Clifford to stay with them several times. Both men were both interested in the Coote Society, an obscure group devoted to proving that Dr Johnson was not in fact the first dictionary-maker. Interested? Rupert had staked his academic reputation on it. In fact, he'd staked their marriage on it. Whatever she'd expected of marriage, this quiet country girl coming for the first time to a huge industrial city and one of its great universities, it hadn't been what she'd got. Rupert had been one of her lecturers, already a man in his middle years. He'd helped her, organised her, demanded her help with his research. And when she'd got her degree — a very good first — he'd married her. And she'd continued with his research. She'd also learned how to manage a surprisingly tight household budget and to button her lip against his constant drip of criticism.

So why — in these days of easy divorce — had she stayed with him? Love? If she'd ever loved him, she certainly hadn't after the first year of marriage. But she'd stayed. And stayed. Well, there'd been nowhere to go, had there? Not for a woman like her, with nothing. Or had she stayed for something? For what? For more contact with Clifford, who had always been charming and debonair, contriving, even as he slept under Rupert's roof, to suggest that one day he and Rebecca should be together? She didn't know. And now she had seen Clifford in quite different circumstances, she knew even less.

CHAPTER
FOUR

End of afternoon school. At last! Tim headed not for the music room and his cello, but for the library. A rescue mission, according to Tony. To tip her the wink that old Swine would be on duty again for early prep. And that she must keep her head down. But equally she must escape when she was supposed to.

"If I know anything of the OB he'll be paying her a pittance," Tony had said. "And he'll screw any extra time out of her he can."

Tim was used to these outbursts against the Chief. He couldn't imagine hating his own father so much. He knew he was supposed to despise him a bit — and he'd learned the hard way that it was best not to be proud of your dad in public. But he could see all the efforts his dad was making. For one thing, busy as he always was, Owen was prepared to write a clever little overture to the school play. Clever not just for the memorable melodies, but for the way he orchestrated it for whatever instruments he had at his disposal. Last year — Tim's first at the school — it had been for wind ensemble. This year it would probably have to be for cello (good job Osric didn't appear till well into the play), piano (Tony) and a rather scratchy violin. Not

23

much of a start for *Hamlet*. Except Dad might have time to come in with the sophisticated keyboards he used himself — he could produce a full orchestra, if he wanted to. Yes, something with impressive kettle-drums . . . That'd suit *Hamlet*.

Mrs Wildbore — where on earth had she got a name like that? — had been busy. From somewhere she'd dug out an ink pad and a date stamp. And that big mess of books was much smaller. Not that putting them on the shelves had made that much difference — there were still acres of bare wood. Though it was a different colour. He could imagine his dad saying sharply, "She's not employed as a cleaner, for heaven's sake!"

She was very dirty. Both her jumper — why on earth had she ever bought such a miserable light browny colour? — and her skirt were due for a wash. And look at her hands. As some point she'd rubbed her nose — there was a long grey streak right across her cheek. And her hair. Bad hair days, they were called, weren't they? This was a dreadful hair day. Oh dear, he had a feeling that if the Chief Master saw her like this she'd be crossed off the list of potential stepmothers for Tony. And he had a feeling Tony liked her. Not that he'd ask. Their friendship was best when they avoided sensitive areas. Such as Tony's mother. She was in the States somewhere. All Tony had said when he'd asked why he didn't go out there to live with her was, "Not with my record."

Mrs W had spotted him and was smiling. He smiled back and headed over to her, finger on lips. He dug in

24

his jacket pocket for the bit of paper he'd written his warning on. It had got more crumpled than he'd expected, and he'd somehow never quite managed to get his handwriting neat. He flushed as he pushed it across the table at her.

She didn't shudder and hold it up between thumb and finger. She opened it carefully, read it and looked up at him. She nodded, and mouthed, "Thanks." She jerked her head in the direction of one of the aisles. "He's there already. Be careful."

But it was too late. Mr Swain was already bearing down on them.

"In trouble again, Griffiths?" The silence rule didn't appear to apply to him. "Passing notes, were we? Thank you for intercepting the missive, Mrs — er — Wildbore. If you give it to me I will see that the punishment fits the crime." And he would no doubt enjoy carrying it out.

Tim bit his lip. But despite the odds Mrs W was keeping her head.

"No, Mr Swain. There's no need for alarm."

What if she referred to him as Tim? They could both be in it!

"The young man — Griffiths, is it? — brought me a note from the Chief Master. A personal message," she added, looking down at the hand out thrust to take it. She produced a coy smile. "Thank you, Griffiths. There is no reply."

He made it as far as the music room corridor before bursting into giggles.

"Whatever else she can do, she can act, that woman," he informed Tony as they headed in for supper. He explained how she'd saved his bacon.

"Bacon! You know, the thought of nice crisp smoked bacon, just like my Ma used to cook it, almost makes me want to turn carnivore again."

Tim gaped.

"No, not while I'm here, at any rate. A thousand and one ways to ruin meat."

Tim shook his head. "No. Just five or six. I think I'll try being a veggie — see if I can get a note from Dad next time he's home. You veggies do better than the rest of us. Couldn't do much worse, though. You ought to tell your dad how bad the grub is."

"You try telling the OB anything. You know, I'm really sorry for that poor cow. She may manage Swine once. But can you see her making a habit of it? Or dealing with Curtis? Or even, God forbid, with the OB? We've got to do something, man. Save her from a fate worse than death."

"You don't mean get her sacked —"

Tony shrugged. "It may just be the best thing for her. In the long run. Let me think about it. God," he said, peering at the servery counter, "grated mousetrap again!"

Back at the cottage Rebecca would have died for crisp bacon and fresh bread. She would even have died for grated mousetrap and fresh bread. But she'd cut so much for her lunch that she had a choice: bread for supper tonight or bread for breakfast tomorrow. Well, there was always porridge for breakfast. But the milk was going off and would probably be undrinkable by the morning. Oh, for the city, and shops open at all hours. She would have to turn to the box of groceries that Margaret, her sister-in-law, had left her as what she'd called iron rations. "No, no need to get anything — anything at all! Leave it to me!" And, in case Rebecca thought it was a house-warming present, a bill was coyly tucked in the top of a packet of cheese biscuits. The meanness of them! Margaret and Rupert both! After all, Margaret knew about the will, and about Rebecca's finances. She'd not commented, but Rebecca had a sense that even Margaret was ashamed of what her brother had done. But when Rebecca had tentatively murmured the words "challenge the will", Margaret had been outraged. "It was Rupert's money and he could do what he liked with it," she'd said, tucking herself into the driving seat of her BMW and turning back towards the motorway.

So Rebecca had had to trail back into the cottage — so cold that when she touched the kitchen wall her hand came away wet — to face her new life here. Alone.

Well, that had been then — was it only thirty-six hours ago? — and tonight was now. She would not go under, Rebecca told herself fiercely. She'd spent what was left of Sunday unpacking the few things she'd brought with her — Clifford had assured her she would need very little, since the cottage was fully equipped — and chopping logs for firewood. At least the little living-room looked more cheerful, the poor lighting combining with the firelight to give an almost cosy effect. Not that the fire raised the temperature all that much. Not even as much as a gas fire — Rupert had never had central heating installed lest it damage his books. But at least — once she'd decided what to eat — she could have her supper on a tray by the flames. No tray? All right. Her supper on a telephone directory by the flames.

So what had Margaret considered essential to life in Devon? Apart from the cheese biscuits which were probably soggy already? Tinned artichoke hearts. Tinned asparagus. Tinned olives. Tinned anchovies. If she could find pasta and olive oil, she could have a real feast. A couple of bottles of wine, with rather scuffed labels: had they been unwelcome party offerings which could be safely passed on? Almond essence. Vanilla essence. Rosewater. Clams. Hundreds and thousands. Baking powder. Marmalade with whisky.

No butter. And no tin-opener in the box or in any of the kitchen drawers.

She could feel her lip trembling. No, she wouldn't give anyone the satisfaction of having reduced her to tears. It was only that she was so hungry. She pulled herself straight. She could have porridge for tea, with the last of the milk, and bread and marmalade for breakfast. And hope the village store opened early enough to get some real food. And a tin-opener.

Meanwhile, she had work to do. With the bleach and the half-bald scrubbing brush left by the last lodger, she was going to scrub the mould from the bathroom tiles. Then at least she could feel it was clean enough to take a bath.

The immersion heater took so long to warm up that she heated the water she needed kettle by heavy kettle. She'd scrubbed the walls almost white and her hands were red raw when it dawned on her: she wasn't ever going to get any hot water from the immersion heater, because the space in the airing cupboard where the hot tank should have been was completely empty.

Towards the end of his early-morning run, Tony saw the small bedraggled figure turning not towards the school but down the hill to the village and quickened his pace to overtake her.

"You're cutting it a bit fine, aren't you, Rebecca?" he called, slowing to a jog.

"I know. But I've got to get some food in."

"The bursar's supposed to have left some."

"The bursar left not so much as a box of matches or a tin-opener," she said tartly.

"But if the OB —"

"OB?"

"Don't ask. Just a nickname. If he spots you coming in late —" He mimed a throat-slitting action.

"What do I do, Tony?"

He couldn't tell whether she was angry or despairing. He waited.

"The shop doesn't open till nine. It closes at twelve thirty. I'm on duty from nine till twelve fifteen — and then some. The shop re-opens at two. I'm due back at the library at one fifteen. The shop closes at five thirty. It was after six when I got away yesterday."

"I thought you were supposed to be part-time," Tony said. "Something to do with employment law, I reckon. The OB and the bursar often seem to take things like that into consideration when drawing up contracts."

"Cheaper and easier to sack, no doubt," she said.

That was what that bastard Swine had been saying to her in the library!

She was looking at her watch. "It's no good, is it? I'd better get back and take pot luck with the school lunch."

"Good idea," he said. "Have you ordered it?" One look at the poor cow's face and he knew she hadn't. Christ, and she was thin enough without skipping meals. She was a bit old to be anorexic, though. "Look," he said, "you zap up there as fast as you can. I'll sweet-talk Mrs Gaye into staying open a bit longer this lunchtime. Shouldn't mind, so long as you escape on time. Go on, Becky. Fast as you can."

"What about you?"

"I'm doing cross-country training, aren't I? Maybe I ran a bit further than I ought — forgot the time or something. Who cares? Just go!"

"You poor love," Mrs Gaye was saying. She was in her early fifties, probably, neat and trim. "Stuck out there in that cold old place. And no food, young Tony was saying."

Brave face time. "Plenty of food. Just the wrong sort. And no tin-opener."

"And no hot water neither. Apart from what you boil. How you going to manage, my dear?" Mrs Gaye leaned comfortable arms on her counter and looked her straight in the eye. "Not fit for human habitation, that place. And the EEC wouldn't let you keep pigs in it, I do know that."

"I've got an appointment with the bursar this afternoon," Rebecca said bravely.

"And are you expecting him to turn water into wine?" Mrs Gaye asked. "Or simply walk on the water — it's damp enough, I'll be bound."

"Just put his hand in his pocket for a new water heater."

Mrs Gaye shook her head. "It'd be easier for him to raise the dead — that don't cost him nothing." And then she added, "Are you sure it's the school that'll pay for it, my dear? They do have a way with small print, some of these accountant folk. You want to make sure you're not landed with a big bill for something you may not want for long. Now, young Tony says you haven't any time to spare, so I've already put a few things together for you. Bread, butter, cheese, tea, milk . . . Oh, and I made you a bit of a sandwich in case you didn't have time to." She ran through them and totted them up on the till.

"Hang on," Rebecca said. "You've missed some things. There's some eggs here. And some runner beans!"

"Well, they'll probably be a bit tough, like, at this end of the year. And as for the eggs, the hens are laying like they're on piece-work. And that there's kindling — you need to make sure that fire of yours starts as soon as you get in, or the place'll be cold as charity."

But it was the warmth of Mrs Gaye's charity that did what nothing else had done so far — reduced Rebecca to tears. She managed to hold them back till she was out of the shop. No. She mustn't give way. She sniffed, and rubbed her nose with the back of her hand.

Before she knew it, kind arms were wrapped round her. "Seems to me you need a nice cup of tea, like, then my George'll run you back. No, no arguing. Young Tony was telling me, you need someone to look after you. Come along in, my dear."

CHAPTER
FIVE

"My dear Mrs Wildbore," the bursar said, showing her into his office and indicating a comfortable chair, "I can't tell you how sorry I am that I've been so remiss. I found the box of groceries in the back of the car this morning! Let me drop it round this evening. Imagine, forgetting that. I can't hope that you'll forgive me. Some tea, anyway." He retreated behind a desk almost, but not quite, as large as Clifford's and pressed a button on his phone. A discreet but probably expensive clock showed four-thirty. Outside the boys would be enjoying physical activities, but the peace of the room wasn't disturbed by yells or shouts. The heavy curtains were already drawn against the uninspiring October sky.

"Thank you." She forced herself to sit back in the chair as if relaxed. At least she no longer felt weak and woozy, thanks to Mrs Gaye's thick ham sandwiches, slices from a homemade malt loaf and good strong coffee, and to the lift back in Mr Gaye's, George's, utility truck. After all that food she'd been ready to fall asleep. How fortunate, she told herself dryly, that she'd had every opportunity to work it off. The pile of unsorted books had now gone altogether, and the shelves were as full as they'd ever be until she'd completed her campaign to have all the outstanding issues returned. And, she hoped, order some more.

"I always like Earl Grey at this time in the afternoon: will that be acceptable?"

Since she'd always had to make do with a second squeeze of the cheapest teabag she could find, it was more than acceptable. She smiled. He looked quite startled, and returned the smile. Dapper men in their late forties did not usually smile at her. She blushed under her dirt, and wondered if he'd still be so polite when she told him the reasons for her appointment with him.

"Do you know Devon at all?" he asked.

So any business they were to discuss would come after the tea.

"Not at all. Apart from the old railway posters. I rather thought it would be warm and sunny." She sounded foolish even to her own ears. "At least, not as cold and wet as this. I don't think it's stopped raining since I arrived!"

"One of the paradoxes of global warming, I'm afraid, Mrs Wildbore. Ah!" He broke off to smile at the woman bringing in a tray. "Have you met my secretary yet? Janice, this is Mrs Wildbore, our new librarian."

The women exchanged cautious smiles. Janice was, if not a fashion-plate, clean and spruce, with a skirt shorter than anything Rebecca had ever worn in her life. Despite the youthful appearance, she was probably a few years older than Rebecca — in her early forties, perhaps.

34

Janice laid the tray where Rebecca could pour, and placed a plate of biscuits where only the bursar could reach them. "Will that be all, Mr Downing?"

"Yes, thanks. We won't want to be interrupted: would you be kind enough to intercept any callers?"

Rebecca couldn't believe such courtesy. Meanwhile, she poured the tea, offered milk or lemon, and passed Downing his cup. He responded by passing the biscuits to her. She could have grabbed the lot. As it was, she confined herself to taking a custard cream, lodging it in the saucer.

She took a deep breath. "There are a couple of things I need, Mr Downing —"

"Oh, Ralph, please!"

"Rebecca," she countered. "First of all, I need a key to the library."

"Of course!" He touched his forehead with the heel of his hand in a gesture of apologetic exasperation. "And one for the lavatories. Lavatory, rather. I'm afraid that in this male preserve such necessities are sadly lacking. The one for women staff is near the gym."

Which implied there must be another, forbidden to the workers? And would someone as chic as Janice be expected to make her way over there? "I couldn't find one at all the other day . . . and I have been getting very dirty."

He didn't actually say, "So I can see," but he might just as well have done. He stared at her in silence. Was he about to offer to pay her cleaning bill? "You're obviously working very hard."

Suppressing a grim laugh, she continued, "I may well need proper stationery supplies. How do I go about getting things like issuing cards?"

He stared at her blankly. "I assume there must be specialised library providers."

"Most libraries are probably computerised these days," she said. "I'm afraid I may have to make do and mend."

"I'll authorise a budget," he said. "So you can chose what you need — oh, get hold of some catalogues — and get them to invoice me." He drank his tea and looked at his watch.

Surprised by such an easy victory, she ate her biscuit before following suit. "Now, there is a much more serious problem," she said. "At the cottage."

He frowned. "Serious?"

"Two things. Someone," she tried to smile, as if they might both find it amusing, "has removed the immersion heater. And the hot water tank. And connected all the taps to the cold water system."

"No. Surely not. People — who would do such a thing? No, Rebecca, you must be —"

"Mistaken? Believe me, Ralph, when you come home from work in my state, you don't make mistakes about hot water. The other thing that worries me is the electric cooker."

"As far as I know it's in full working order."

"Perhaps you'd care to check when you come round tonight. With the groceries," she added, as he looked quite blank.

Something told her she wouldn't be offered another biscuit. Nor was she.

"All I hope is that he won't make her cry," Tim said, falling into step with Tony on the patch of tarmac Payne-in-the-Arse called the Quad. "Sarcky bugger."

Tony considered. "Downing? No, he'll smile."

"Like the man in *Hamlet*? Smiling and smiling and being a villain?"

"Who's been mugging up for the auditions, then?" Tony aimed a playful punch at Tim's shoulder. "No, I don't see you as Claudius, kid. Look, there she is. And she doesn't seem to be crying."

"Not outside, maybe," Tim said, earning a surprised glance from Tony. "I mean, she's got — got —"

"Chutzpah? You know, pzazz. Well, she hasn't got it anyway."

"Never said she had. But I reckon she's got — pride, or something. You know," Tim pulled himself into a parody of erectness, "stiff upper lip and all that."

"They'll recruit her into the STC, then. Why d'you say that?" Tony asked, interested.

"Just the way she looks at someone and you can tell she's thinking something but she doesn't say it."

"More fool her. That's the way to get walked all over, if you ask me. And I'd say that's what she is. Down-trodden. Put upon. Whatever. Come on, why else would she be here?"

"Money?"

Tony tapped Tim's head. "Anything in here? Come on, Tim. She wants money, she doesn't work here."

"Perhaps — perhaps she's lost all her money and —"

"She'd go off to the DSS."

"No, perhaps someone's run away with it and —"

"She'd go to the police, sort out her insurance. Get real, kid." But maybe Tim was on to something. Tony was silent as they headed indoors and strolled down to the music room. Why on earth had his father brought her here? Old Bastard couldn't really be in love with her, could he? He thought of the other women his father had bedded — all naff in some way or other. Most had too much make-up, clothes too young. God knows where he'd picked them up. None of them was mother material, anyway. Hell, he'd been so stupid getting caught with those Es. He didn't even use the bloody things. Too dangerous by half. Who wanted to pop bloody cow anaesthetic to get a kick? Anyway, possession of a class A drug — even one you're looking after for a mate in case he gets picked up — is not the sort of thing to endear you to US Immigration. Or an ex-Marine Corps stepfather. And no, he didn't write to his mother saying come and rescue me from this stuffed shirt of a father. He wrote and told her how hard he was working. Bloody right he was working hard. That way escape lay!

"I said, guitar and drums or cello and piano?" Tim was saying, exasperated.

"Oh!" He looked down at Tim. There was no doubt which he preferred, however hard he pretended to be macho and king of the group. "How about playing with the thing between your legs you sit and stroke . . ."

Rebecca's hands were so cold she could scarcely strike the match. And she was desperate for even the inadequate heat of the fire. But then she paused. Why not let her visitor have the full effect of her new home? He'd said he'd be here by five forty — he was dropping by on his way home. Only another minute or two. What she couldn't work out was why she hadn't had the sense to ask him for a lift. She wouldn't have minded waiting — anything to escape the thin, miserable drizzle that had replaced the rain.

Keeping her coat on, she busied herself unpacking the bags Mrs Gaye had packed for her. To Mrs Gaye's obvious consternation, she'd had to add packet soups and tinned vegetables to the more wholesome supplies.

"The trouble is," she'd said, by way of excuse — more explanation, really — "I'm not sure how much of the stove is actually working. Not that I'm not much of a cook." She might have been, once. But Rupert had never noticed what she put before him, provided it was what he called "good, plain cooking — meat and two vegetables." Which was, of course, a good deal more expensive than the pasta or rice-based recipes she used to cut from the newspapers — until he decided he didn't have time to read them and cancelled them. It would be such a joy — once she'd broken the back of the library work — to steal quiet minutes with a good newspaper once more. And copy out some promising recipes.

By hand, of course. How could a school library function these days without a photocopier? And how would her suggestion that they get one be received? She could imagine the very expressions on the faces of Clifford and the bursar! For the first time since she could remember, she threw her head back and laughed.

It was after seven when she heard a car draw up outside the cottage and footsteps approach the front door. Then there was silence. Finally, just as she was getting anxious, there was a knock on the front door. Or a kick. It sounded much more like a kick.

It probably was a kick. Ralph Downing was standing on her doorstep, his arms occupied with a cardboard box.

"Your bell's not working," he said, as if it were her fault. He stepped inside without bothering to wipe his feet. She might have risked protesting, but the carpet was so filthy a few more marks would make little difference. He looked round for somewhere to dump his burden.

She opened the kitchen door. "On the table, please."

"So where's this cooker?" he asked.

She pointed — not that there was any way he could miss it in a kitchen this size.

He peered at the red adhesive tape covering three of the red-ring control knobs with interest. "Why has that been put there?"

"It was there when I arrived," she said. "I didn't know whether it was to indicate they weren't working or to warn the user of potential electrocution." Perhaps she had one thing to be grateful to Rupert for: she could turn on his dry, pedantic speech when she needed to.

Downing half turned to her. "Well, I can't do anything. Try them and see."

"While I'm standing on a damp stone floor?" She shook her head. Rupert's implacable gesture. It worked.

"Oh, there must be someone in the village who could repair it. Right, I'd better be off, then." He headed out of the kitchen.

"The airing-cupboard's in the bathroom upstairs," she said.

"I really haven't time —"

"I really haven't any hot water. Nor any means of heating cold water."

He shrugged, taking care not to let his Barbour brush against the wallpaper on the steep and narrow stairs. She didn't follow him.

"Hmm," he said, coming down almost immediately. "You really should make an effort to air this place. You mustn't encourage damp. We'll be getting structural problems if you're not careful."

"I think you've got damp," she said. "The trouble is, there's no means of heating it, as far as I can see."

He drew himself up to his full six feet, "Mrs Wildbore, there was nothing in your contract to say we'd nanny you with heaters. You must have equipment like that of your own."

"Mr Clifford-Payne," she began, pleased she'd remembered the official name, "said the cottage was fully equipped and — and — advised me not to bring anything." That sounded dreadfully lame. But how could she admit that Clifford had threatened her with legal action if she removed anything from her house?

41

"Not on my behalf, my dear Rebecca. But as a trustee of the Coote Society, I must protect its interests. And the will quite clearly says that the house and contents must be sold for the benefit of what was, after all, Rupert's lifelong passion."

It did sound lame. Quite clearly. She took a deep breath. Now was not the time to cry again.

"In any case," she said, reverting to Rupert-speak, "I would hesitate to use any electrical appliance until the wiring has been checked."

A flicker of his eye said he would too. But he said, "I really can't see any cause for your alarm. But I will authorise the school maintenance man to call when he's next on the premises."

"Which will be?"

He stared.

"Whenever his schedule permits. Now, Mrs Wildbore, I really cannot keep you any longer." He opened the front door, slamming it behind him. Or rather, trying to slam it. The wood was so warped it took several attempts.

And once again Rebecca found herself laughing.

CHAPTER
SIX

Wednesday morning. And there was something strange about the early-morning light. Rebecca pulled her dressing-gown from the pile of clothes she'd heaped on the bed to augment the thin blankets. Still in bed, she shuffled her arms into it. Only then did she emerge.

Sun! And suddenly she realised why everyone raved about Devon. The moors — seeming now so close she could reach and touch them — were purple in the autumn sun. The nearer fields were either golden with harvest stubble or still verdant for the sheep and cattle. Yes, the leaves were dropping fast, but they were the colours she'd once painted back in the Welsh Marches. This morning it was good to be alive.

Despite the school. Despite the cottage.

And this afternoon was free. The boys would be playing rugby. She — yes, she would start on that wilderness of a garden. She'd ask the locals what to plant. Broad beans. They were best over-wintered, weren't they? Suddenly, she knew she could do anything.

The first thing to do was to stow away the groceries the bursar had been so good as to bring. OK, his efforts to leave with dignity had been funny enough. But she'd ended so cold and so miserable trying — and failing — to get damp wood to start a fire she'd had to give up. She'd made up one of those packet soups on the only red-ring without red tape, longed for toast and settled for bread, and headed for bed. Via the chilly bathroom and a chillier all-over wash. Her hair had taken for ever to dry. Goodness knew what it would look like this morning,

The sun was streaming in through the kitchen window, making the place warmer than she'd known it. And also more depressing. Every stain, every bit of chipped paint, every layer of dirt was put under its spotlight. She'd have to repaint it. And she was all too aware that Clifford had told her that redecoration — in the unlikely event of any being needed — was her responsibility. And at her expense.

A thought shot into her head. Was there any point if she didn't intend to stay there?

And then, looking at the crack spreading across the old crock sink, she knew she had no choice. Not as things stood.

Not as things stood.

Briskly — she still had to go into school, didn't she? — she filled the kettle and set it on the red-ring. Porridge? There was no doubt it was good for you. Better than the selection of individual cereals that the bursar had brought. What else was there? She would compare his selection with Margaret's and award points.

For originality Margaret's won hands down. The bursar went for bulk. Things, that is, to make his offering look larger than it was. Kitchen towels and loo roll — family pack. Washing powder — fine when she had an automatic machine to use it in. At least he hadn't been crass enough to buy dishwasher powder. Paper tissues. Family-size shampoo. Family-size shower gel! Imagine, the luxury of a hot shower! Apart from that, baked beans, a huge tub of cheap margarine, a bag of pudding rice and a tub of custard powder. At the bottom of the bag — yes, she'd guessed! — was the bill, discreetly tucked into a pack of scouring pads. She was ready to laugh again. And then couldn't resist. Tesco's gave you not just the total and the till. But the time when it was bought. Six twenty, the previous evening.

The lane looked as if it had been washed in blood where the rich soil had been soaked from the banks. Would she meet Tony on one of his runs, this morning? It would be nice to have some company. No. If he were running, he wouldn't want to bother with her. She hoped Tim didn't hero-worship him too much, though it would be easy to: in his shorts and tracksuit top, Tony had looked imposing. Glamorous, even, with the rain glistening in his dark curly hair and making his leg muscles gleam. Above all alive, in a way that drove her to quicken her step. Once she'd been young and fit, lithe and full of life. Now look at her. Scruffy, unkempt, badly turned out: whatever expression she chose, things only got worse. And there was nothing she could do about it. To be smart, you needed money, so you didn't have to haunt factory-seconds and charity shops on special reductions days. And to get money, you had to work. She was unqualified, as Rupert had constantly reminded her, for anything in this modern world. Her degree was out of date, she had no special skills, she couldn't even be a teacher unless she took a course. Clifford, shaking his head sadly, had been forced — when Rupert put it to him — to agree. Which was why his offer of both work and accommodation had been so generous. Indeed, providential.

Her thoughts were interrupted by the sound of running feet and hard breathing. She turned in delight. But it wasn't Tony. It was Jeremy Cavendish. He slowed to a jog and fell into step with her.

Sweat was trickling down his face and neck, and turning his blond hair dark at the roots. His was the sort of complexion that darkened into brick-red as he got hot. "And how are you, this bright and beautiful morning?" he asked.

"Fine," she said positively. "It's so nice to see some sun, isn't it? Almost like summer!"

"You wait till you turn that bend," he said, pointing ahead. "Then you'll know what season it is! Can't stop, or I'll catch my death. See you later, maybe!"

She watched him as he gathered speed, suddenly desolate in a patch where the sun hadn't reached. Once she'd been able to laugh and joke with attractive young men. Now it seemed she'd lost even that skill.

As he came into the library, Tony flapped an idle hand in Rebecca's direction, but made no attempt to come over. Instead, he grabbed a paper from the table she'd found to arrange them on, a neatly hand-printed notice reminding readers to return them, folded in the proper order, as soon as they'd finished them. Each was stamped — authoritatively but optimistically — DO NOT REMOVE FROM THE LIBRARY.

That would stop the masters. He didn't think.

Old Sowerby was shuffling over to Rebecca's table even now. The trouble was he insisted on wearing his suits until they were too tatty even for a charity shop, with precious few visits to the cleaner's. Every year, he committed one outfit to the flames — on the Guy! He tended to adopt, as his shoes went the way of his suits, a shuffling walk. The result was that no one could tell he was a teacher. A good teacher, too. The best Tony had come across. God knows what he was doing teaching Classics in a dump like this. Couldn't face moving his collection of prize cacti to some other place, maybe. And he was almost certainly too old to find another school to take him on. If any other schools did Classics these days.

There, Rebecca was looking up and smiling at the old guy. He was bowing in his half-courtly, half-sycophantic way. No clues there for her. And now he was gesturing around at the shelves, running a finger along the nearest and showing her the tip. Clean, almost certainly, after the way she'd flogged herself the last couple of days. But now she was showing him the radiator. Yes! She thought Sowerby was the caretaker! He slipped the *Guardian* back in place and lounged quietly nearer.

"Ah, Mrs Wildbore, I do hope you haven't tried to adjust this."

The poor woman blushed: she must have had a go, and why not? It was bloody cold over here.

"With the wind in this direction, you must have been tempted. Allow me. One turn in this direction, do you see, and half a turn back. That's the idea. Please note the position now. Perhaps you should mark it."

She gently eased him upright before bending herself and solemnly applying a pencil to the valve.

"Thank you, Mrs Wildbore. Now, these missing books. May I suggest you turn your attention to the staff room? Hmm? A shabby crew, some of these young men. A shabby crew. Now, good day to you. And remember, one turn forward, half a turn back." And off he shuffled.

Tony followed. "Rehearsing for Polonius, Sir?" he asked brightly, once they were through the doors.

He was rewarded by a twinkle, and a finger touched to the lips. "A harmless jest, Tony."

Tony looked him straight in the eye. "Do you reckon she'll see it that way? When she finds out who you are?"

"She's nothing to reproach herself for! Her behaviour was what we used to call perfectly ladylike."

"But she was taken in something shocking, wasn't she? And I've an idea she's been taken in by other people, too."

"You mean —"

"By the Chief Master, for one."

"Your father, Tony," Sowerby said firmly.

"By the Chief Master," Tony repeated, equally firmly. "God knows what he told her about the place and God knows what he's paying her."

48

Sowerby coughed gently. "I understand she doesn't have any qualifications, Tony. She's probably grateful to get respectable work."

Tony pulled his chin. "She doesn't talk like someone with no qualifications. And it's not the pay that worries me. It's that cottage. They never bothered to do it up after they got rid of the squatter."

"You could hardly call that poet a squatter."

"Well, he might not have done any real damage. But him being there meant the — the Chief Master didn't have to spend anything on the place, didn't it? And I can't imagine bloody Downing wanting to spend any money. He looks after the school dosh as if it's his own."

"As he ought. But I'm sorry if I've made an unhappy young woman more unhappy. I'll contrive some apology." Sowerby nodded and shuffled off.

Tim didn't know whether to roar with laughter or go and bollock old Sowerby. Tony convinced him that the latter was not on. "Apart from anything else, he would think that what he was saying to me was confidential. And I fancy the poor old bugger's quite upset. Leave him to sort it."

"What if he doesn't?"

"We put plan B into operation."

"What's plan B?"

"No idea."

They fell into a friendly scuffle.

So what was George Gaye's utility doing parked outside her cottage? Rebecca walked even more briskly, calling and waving. Despite the shoes, which had stretched so badly she was in danger of losing them, she broke into a run. But he wouldn't be driving away because he wasn't in the cab.

She heaved open the gate, and followed his trail — he'd pushed through the overgrown weeds into the back garden.

"George?"

He turned and smiled, a big man in comparison with his wife, and a good deal greyer. His Devon burr was stronger too. "Ah, I've been having a look at this roof of yours, my dear. Not very clever, is it? And I reckon we should get some of that creeper off the wall — it might look nice but you may be getting some problems with damp!"

"Getting! Got, more like! You come and see inside."

To her amazement he fished a key from under an overflowing water-butt. "Oh, everyone knows it's there. But I didn't like to go in without you being there — wouldn't want you to think I'd been prying in your things."

"Nothing to pry in, George. But thanks for waiting for me. What can I do for you, anyway? Mrs Gaye all right?"

"She's making jam this afternoon — happy as a pig in muck. No, it's not what you can do for me, so much as what I can do for you. I do all the maintenance work for the school, see. Part-time. So Mr Downing asked me to drop down when I had a moment. Now, my day for school work is Mondays. But — well, you were a bit upset yesterday, weren't you? And I thought it might be something to do with this place."

He opened the back door and stood aside to let her go in first. "My heavens!" He recoiled as the smell rolled out. "You were right about that damp, my dear. Now," he got out a notepad and, fishing his pencil from behind his ear, licked the point. Rebecca had never seen anyone do that before. It was hard not to giggle.

"Fire away," he said.

"Cooker." She filled the kettle and put it on the one red-ring.

"My lord. Be one Noah threw out of his Ark, that one. Oh, I don't like the thought of you using that, my dear. Tell you what, me and Mary have got this old camping stove — two burners, works on bottled gas. It'd just fit on the top of that. Until the school gets you something better."

He worked his way through the rest of the cottage, exclaiming and murmuring under his breath.

At last, a mug of tea in his hand, he sat at the kitchen table. He looked very serious. "By rights I reckon this place should be condemned."

He was right, wasn't he? But what would happen to her without even this shelter? "I don't want that. I've nowhere else to go!"

He looked at her very kindly. "Well, what we got to do is make it sound as if we can make it decent without costing his nibs too much. 'Cause if he thinks it's going to cost, I reckon —"

"That he'll find some excuse to sack me — so he can throw me out of here?" she said very calmly.

"That's what they call a worst-case scenario, isn't it, my dear? Well, remember, I do all the work at the school. And if old George can't find some of the things you need, and fiddle some others with a bit of clever figure work, he isn't the man he thinks he is. Trouble is, my dear, it'll take time, doing it secret like. Can you wait that long?"

Rebecca smiled sadly. "I'm afraid, as the lady said, 'There Is No Alternative!'"

Did she hear herself add the word "yet" under her breath?

CHAPTER
SEVEN

Rebecca had hardly started on the garden when George reappeared.

"Look, my dear, you'll get your hands all mucked up if you're not careful. My Mary's sent these." He produced a pair of thick leather gauntlets. "And the wellies — she thought you and she were much of a size. No, she won't be wanting them back today. Remember: it's her jam-making this afternoon. And I thought this spade'd be a lot better than that wobbly old thing they left behind. And this here's a machete — now, you be careful what you're doing with that, but you'll find it great for those old brambles. Now, remember, don't you try and do it all at once. When the Lord made time, He made plenty of it. Right?"

"And when the Lord made work, He made plenty of that!" she countered, laughing.

She'd walked with him as far as the utility. George was the sort of man you could ask a favour of. And if he couldn't help, he'd say so. "George — when you next go into Newton Abbot or Exeter — provided it's not in school-time, I mean — would you give me a lift? Only the buses don't run too often, and I want to get some cheap emulsion — anything to cheer up the place a bit."

"I'll give you a lift any time you want, my dear. But don't you go worrying about buying paint. Especially cheap paint. That won't cover what you've got to cover. No, with paint, you get what you pay for."

Despite herself, her face fell.

"No need to let the clouds come down, either. As if old George can't find you some paint! School property, school paint. Obvious."

She shook her head. "It says in my contract I'm responsible for any redecoration."

"Who says anything about redecoration? Nothing "re" about it! Now, I've got white and I've got magnolia. Which d'you fancy? I have to say, I think white's a bit stark. And there's no doubting magnolia would cover better."

She clutched her forehead as if making a tough decision. "I don't know . . . Hard isn't it? OK — let's go for magnolia."

"Good girl. Now, what I want to know is," he said, dropping his voice and looking around, "has the Gaffer ever been down here? And is he likely to come?"

"I've no idea. Why?"

"Because when the staff room was re-carpeted they used quite good-quality stuff. Well, all that wear and tear, even Mr Downing had to admit they needed it. And I was thinking, the off-cuts would be just big enough — not for your living-room, I'm afraid — but at least for your bedroom."

"You know, George," she said, "I don't somehow think Mr Clifford-Payne will ever be coming into my bedroom."

She was laughing, but he nodded, very seriously. "I'm glad to hear that, my dear. Because there's this rumour going round the village that you're — well, let's say you're very close, you two. There's even some who say you're going to wed."

"And people don't think that's a very good idea?"

He looked at her closely again. "Do you, my dear?"

Tim had been waiting outside Payne-in-the-Arse's office for five minutes. At least. And although he wasn't shitting himself with fright, he certainly wasn't happy. He'd been racking his brain to remember what he could have done to deserve the official summons, but couldn't come up with anything. Nothing worse than usual, at least.

"Come!"

At last. He opened the door gently, closed it equally gently, and took two steps forward. Then he stopped, standing at rigid attention.

"Ah. Griffiths." P.A. nodded, and, putting on those silly half-moon glasses, looked down at a pile of files on his desk. He found one, rejected it, and found another. "Your father, Griffiths."

Tim's stomach turned to water. He'd never let on — not even to Tony — how scared he was by flying. And especially by his father's flying. There'd been a crash, hadn't there? *Dad was missing*. And he'd have to identify the charred body.

The Chief was waiting.

He had to lick his lips, to swallow. "Yes — yes, Sir."

"A telephone message."

Tim shut his eyes.

"To tell you — yes, here is his message — that he should be returning to the United Kingdom earlier than planned and that, while he hopes you will remain here for the duration of Saturday, he would like me to grant you an exeat for Sunday."

God, he'd wet himself if he wasn't careful. Or throw up.

"Now, I will agree on this one occasion, but I do expect you, Griffiths, to adhere in future to the more usual arrangement. In other words, either you are at home for the weekend, or you are here. Is that clear?"

"Sir."

"I will put this in writing to your father. You will deliver the letter when you see him on Sunday."

"Yes, Sir. Thank you, Sir."

"Now, Griffiths." P.A. took off his glasses. "I understand that you are spending a great deal of time on your music."

He wanted to be a professional musician — wasn't he supposed to practise? "Sir."

"I do not want to hear it said that you are neglecting your other studies."

"Sir."

"Are you up-to-date in your work?"

"Sir." The bastard — any of the masters could have told him that.

56

"Good. So I hear. But I do hear of a certain lack of enthusiasm for sport?"

"Sir?"

"Rugby practice, Griffiths. Last to appear, first to leave, I hear."

Only last week, when he'd been on an errand for Swine. Not the sort of man to take rugger as an excuse ... And he'd been early, today. He'd only left in response to P.A.'s summons.

"Not good enough. Team sports build *esprit de corps*, Griffiths."

No point in trying to explain to the bugger that he'd bowl his heart out all day, but hated rugger. The mud. Sweaty bodies. His hands under studded boots ...

"Sir."

"I don't want to hear this complaint again, Griffiths. Understood?"

"Sir."

P.A. picked up his glasses and read through the file again.

Tim knew better than to move, although his bladder was now bursting.

At last, at long last, he knew P.A would lift his head, blink slowly, as if to ask, *And what are you doing? Still here, cluttering up my room*? And make a flapping gesture with his hand, as if wafting away a bad smell.

Tony was just coming out of the bogs as Tim dashed in. He'd better wait. Curtis was in one of the cubicles, and he wanted to make sure Tim wasn't harassed. Or worse.

At last Tim reappeared. "Hi, Tony," he said, his face lighting up like a Halloween head.

Silly kid. No wonder there were rumours about them being lovers. One thing was for sure, the rumour-mongers didn't know Tony. He couldn't remember ever once having fancied a boy, though there'd been plenty of older boys after him when he'd been Tim's age. Definitely hetero. But he was very fond of Tim. As if he was a kid brother. The kid brother he'd never known, and who was living in the States, with Ma and the stepfather.

"You all right, kid? I thought you were going to spew or something."

Tim looked at his feet.

"Old Bastard been bothering you? Come on, spit it out. Look we both know he's a bastard. Maybe I'm a foundling, or something! He and Ma really did find me under a gooseberry bush!"

Tim managed a pale smile. "He just called me in to tell me Dad's coming home earlier than planned. But the way he said it — I thought Dad — well . . . It's silly, isn't it? I thought there'd been a plane crash and —"

God, the kid was nearly in tears! What he needed was a good hug — one thing he certainly couldn't have in a place like this!

"Look, Tim, when was the last time you came for a run?"

"We've just had rugger, Tony!"

"Rugger's rugger and a run's a run. Clears the head. Go on. Get changed. Better make it tracksuit. I'll see you in the Quad in ten minutes."

It was more of a jog, really. The poor kid was knackered after his afternoon on the playing field. Tony took him a short and easy route, which would take them back up the school drive and back to base. And, incidentally, past Rebecca's cottage.

Rebecca wiped her sleeve across her forehead and straightened. Oh, for a hot bath! She'd suffer for this, tomorrow. But at least she could see good, rich, red earth. She'd even dug over a patch some two yards square. Not just to prove she could. More to give her muscles a break from slashing the brambles and weeds. Thank goodness for the Gayes — their tools and their gloves. When she'd cleaned off the worst of the mud, she'd stroll down into the village to return them.

As she drew breath, she realised she wasn't alone. A robin was inspecting her efforts. And a couple of blackbirds. What a cliché! All it needed was for the robin to perch on her spade. Which he duly did.

Laughing, she kicked off the wellies outside the backdoor. And caught the sound of fists on her front door. Who on earth? But she couldn't miss the chance of a visitor and scuttled through in her stockinged feet.

"Hi!"

It was Tim! And behind him Tony!

"Hi, both of you!" What could she say? *What do you want*? How about, "What brings you here? Apart from your feet!" She stepped back, as if to invite them in.

They stepped forward. Tim stopped, bringing Tony to an abrupt halt. "Trainers," he said, unlacing them.

"Ah. Trainers. But pretty smelly feet," Tony said, following suit.

"What's a couple of pairs of sweaty feet — three pairs, counting mine — compared with —" She shut up. Tony didn't have all that much respect for his father but he might not like having him criticised in front of a younger boy.

"Phew, what a pong," Tim said. "What on earth is it, Mrs W?"

"That, my son, is damp," Tony said grimly.

What now? They were her guests. She ought to offer them something. "Do sit down. Would you like a coffee? Or tea?"

"Caffeine's not a good idea if you're exercising, thanks, Rebecca."

"Fruit juice?" Tim suggested, with a slight, anxious frown.

"Sorry. I haven't any. And the only biscuits I've got are cheese and probably soggy already. I'm so sorry . . ."

"No problem," said Tony, solving the problem by getting to his feet. "We only dropped by to say, 'hi'. Which we did!"

What a nice young man! She responded to his cheeky grin with a smile of her own. She turned to Tim, whose face was suddenly transformed by a grin to match Tony's.

The cottage seemed very empty when they'd gone.

What she didn't expect, when she turned up at the Gayes', was to be turned round and sent back.

"You go and get a change of clothes, my dear," Mrs Gaye told her. "You won't want to put them back on, not after a nice hot bath. No, no argufying. I've got the water heater on already. Off you pop. And there's a nice bit of chicken roasting for supper. One George reared himself. And he'd be mightily offended if you didn't stay . . ."

CHAPTER
EIGHT

Tim was just scanning the headlines when Curtis stalked into the library. Shit! And there was no Tony to dash in to the rescue. It was all up to him! Trying to look casual, he abandoned the paper and did his best to sidle nearer without appearing to sidle anywhere.

If she saw him, Mrs W gave no hint of it. She gave no hint of seeing Curtis, either, as she got to her feet to check something in a filing cabinet drawer. A filing cabinet! How'd she got hold of one of those? He must tell Tony!

Since her back was towards him, Curtis had to attract her attention. How would he do it? Tim was fascinated. She was using tactics! And she was winning. Curtis had a note, and laid it briefly on Mrs W's table. Then he seemed to think better of it, and picked it up.

"Note for you," he said aloud at last. "I said, note for you."

Mrs W might not have heard the first time, but she couldn't have missed hearing the second. She did nothing, though, still intent on that filing cabinet drawer.

At last, in her own good time, she shut the drawer and turned back to the table, giving an exaggerated little jump as she saw Curtis.

"Oh, I do beg your pardon."

What was she doing apologising to the creep? But she hadn't finished.

"I thought I heard someone speak but I couldn't believe anyone would violate the silence rule. Unless it were an urgent errand, of course." All the time, her face was straight.

"I've got a note, Miss." Curtis put it on the table.

"*Mrs* Wildbore." She smiled, holding out her hand.

Curtis — if only Tim could see his face! — must have been fuming. But he had to pick it up and hand it to her.

"Thank you. Now, would you be kind enough to wait while I see if I need to reply."

The poor bugger had to, didn't he!

She opened the envelope — envelope! — and pulled out a sheet of paper. She read it and nodded. "No — I won't detain you any longer — Curtis, is it?"

It was almost as if she were acting the role of Payne-in-the-Arse! Tim waited a couple of minutes before toddling over. Since Cavendish was just coming through the door, he couldn't say anything. He just gave a thumbs up gesture and winked. She did the same. Funny thing was, her hand was shaking. She stuck it, and the other one, into her pockets as Cavendish came up. Tim thought it best to beat it.

"Tony!" It was Rebecca.

He stopped and turned. Silly woman, calling like that after him when everyone could hear. She was supposed to call him "Payne", wasn't she? "Clifford-Payne," if the OB were around.

Her face fell. "I'm sorry."

All he'd done was frown a bit. Though that did make him look horribly like the OB.

"No, you're all right. What's the problem?"

"Just some advice, please. Your father has invited me to supper tonight —" Tony whistled — had he indeed?

"He says in his note I need not reply if I can go. I have a feeling he'd expect me to anyway."

"You feel right," he said. "Best handwriting, too. And" — could he say it, without embarrassing her? — "and best bib and tucker, too. Although the note probably says 'informal'. But don't go overboard, eh?"

"You don't mean I should leave the tiara at home! Oh, Tony! I am so disappointed."

"Yeah, shame, isn't it!" He returned her grin. "Look, I've got to dash. See you!" And he left her where she stood. Not good, that. Not much style, Tony old lad. So he set off as if he really were late for something.

So what was he to do about this evening? The OB had been known to spring these suppers on him, expecting him to make up the numbers. So though he'd had no warning of it yet, that didn't mean he wouldn't be bidden, too. And he was buggered if he'd go and watch the OB spooning the charm over that poor cow. He was well on the way to convincing Rebecca that the OB was to be avoided at all costs. But the woman was susceptible — might make all sorts of silly commitments if he wasn't there to cool things.

And if she wasn't sweet and compliant, then she could be well and truly in the shit. The OB wasn't the sort of man to take rejection — of any sort — lying down. Somehow he'd got to manage to avoid the meal but be floating round the house immediately after it. He'd better give it some thought now . . .

"No, handling Curtis is one thing. Handling the Old Bastard's quite another." Tony shoved his hands into his pockets and leaned against the music room wall.

"What about handling Cavendish, then? I tell you, he was looking at her as if he was going to eat her."

"No. Look, Tim, he prefers his tottie young and cuddly. With big knockers."

"I tell you, he's sniffing after her. What are we going to do?"

"Let him sniff. They're adults. Much the same age. Let them have a damned good fuck if they want," Tony said, irritated he couldn't contain his anger, and even more irritated knowing that while Tim wouldn't say anything about it, he'd notice all the same.

"What if she gets involved with him? I wouldn't want her to get hurt."

"You sound like Mrs Gaye: '*I wouldn't want her to get hurt*.' He mimicked Mrs Gaye's burr.

"Well, I wouldn't. She's a nice woman and Cavendish is a big prick."

Tony snorted. "Quite a small one actually. According to my sources. Now, isn't it time we got stuck — ooh!

Pardon my French! — into that Brahms?" Which would give him time to work out how to deal with this evening.

Rebecca handed her coat and scarf to a toothy woman dressed in black who introduced herself as Mr Clifford-Payne's housekeeper. Rebecca thought for one melodramatic moment the woman said her name was Mrs Danvers, but it turned out to be Daniels. Not that she looked ominous, more comic, in a sad sort of way. If Rebecca had lost weight since she'd last worn her black dress, Mrs Daniels had plainly gained it. And the light-weight black tights she favoured did no more for her varicose veins than the high-heeled shoes did for her bunions or her posture. But at least she was affable, commenting on the cold of the evening, the amount of rain they'd had and . . .

What Rebecca could detect above her chatter was the sound of another woman's voice. She managed not to heave a sigh of relief. Thank goodness she wouldn't have to spend the evening tête-à-tête with Clifford — or, worse, perhaps, with Clifford and with Tony, which would probably have been just as uncomfortable, if in a different way. Would Tony bother to conceal his hostility, indeed contempt, for his father? Whom, of course, he never referred to except by his title or as the OB. And she wasn't sure her own acting skills were up to pretending that she hardly knew the young man.

"My dear Rebecca," Clifford said, breaking off in mid-sentence as Mrs Daniels announced her. He set aside his sherry glass the better to get to his feet. If the movement wasn't graceful it was gallant, as was the air-kiss to her right cheek. Taking her by the hand, he led her forward. "Allow me to present Mrs Rebecca Wildbore to you, Sowerby. Rebecca, Reginald Sowerby, Head of Classics."

The old man in the greenish DJ stood up. He was horribly familiar. He had the grace to look embarrassed. "Mrs Wildbore." He bowed over her hand.

Rebecca nearly laughed. She couldn't stop the broadest of smiles.

"Do I gather that you already know each other?" Clifford asked stiffly.

"We met in the library the other day. Mr Sowerby was very helpful."

"Indeed?"

"A trifling matter, Chief Master. Mrs Wildbore gives me too much credit." But the old man's smile was very warm and, as he sat down, he patted the place beside him on the sofa.

"And Mr and Mrs Cowley."

They shook hands. Mr Cowley was a dry-looking man in his late fifties, perhaps, his DJ enlivened by a foppish red-silk handkerchief drooping from his breast pocket. Mrs Cowley, a walking warning to all middle-aged women who dye their hair over-bright gold, exposed a foolish amount of crepey bosom.

Five of them altogether. She'd have expected Clifford to be punctilious about even numbers sitting down to dine: please, don't let him draft in Tony as a spare body! But no, that would have meant too many men, so when they sat to their meal, Mrs Daniels joined them.

All very civilised. And, apart from Mr Sowerby's low and scurrilous observations, the next hour and a half was so dull, she might have welcomed even the presence of Tony to enliven things.

Well, the food was plentiful. She had to admit that. A thick vegetable soup. Then roast beef with all the trimmings. Bigger portions for the men than for the women, she couldn't help noticing. Vegetables rather overcooked by her standards. But the pudding — definitely not a mere sweet — was wonderful, provided it left her fillings intact. Treacle sponge. Magic. And then cheese and biscuits. After all her years of small meals, what she really needed was a doggy bag. Or even a large napkin in which to hide a week's worth of protein.

It seemed it was still the custom here for the ladies to withdraw, leaving the gentlemen to their port and racy conversation. Mrs Daniels coughed demurely and caught first her eyes then Mrs Cowley's. They stood, with such giggly grace that Rebecca was tempted to drop a Lizzie Bennet curtsey. Mrs Cowley headed straight for the lavatory. Mrs Daniels graciously offered Rebecca a tour of the establishment.

She might have expected to see the kitchen, the study, the guest rooms upstairs — Rupert must have slept in that satin-swathed bed! — but when Mrs Daniels threw open the door of a room she declared to be Antony's room, Rebecca was appalled.

"No — please." This was Tony's territory — admission surely by invitation only.

68

"Such an obliging young man," Mrs Daniels was saying. "Look, a place for everything and everything in its place."

It could have been a hotel room, it was so characterless. No books, no posters, no teenage mess. Rebecca backed out the instant she could. No, at least she was spared the embarrassment of being discovered there. She didn't know whether to be amused or irritated not to be shown Clifford's bedroom — "En-suite bathroom, of course" — or Mrs Daniels' own poor domain.

If only the room had been candle-lit, the after-dinner scene in the drawing-room might also have come straight from Jane Austen. Mrs Daniels produced a sewing-box and tapestry frame and Clifford a pack of cards. Rebecca was clearly expected to seat herself at the piano and play light music to entertain them all.

Instead, saying, quite truthfully, that the piano really wasn't her instrument, she sat rather close to the door, and prayed for a an excuse to be on her way. The conversation from the bridge-players was perfunctory, that from Mrs Daniels effusive. But there was a distinct undercurrent that Rebecca could only attribute to resentment that she was about to unseat the older woman. Since Rebecca could hardly deny it, her part in the conversation was limited.

She pricked her ears as she heard whistling in the hall. So did Clifford.

"Antony!" he called. "Is that you, Antony?"

A head round the door proved that that was the case. Tony nodded politely at everyone. He was obviously about to back out again when Clifford called him back.

"Antony, I presume you are about to return to School House for the night."

"Sir."

Sir! To his own father!

"I wonder . . . Mrs Wildbore has had a long and busy day and I'm afraid we have nowhere near finished this rubber. Would you be kind enough to escort her to the safety of her cottage? One cannot be too careful, with this prowler around."

"Certainly, Sir. Mrs Wildbore?"

Playing the moment as if Mr Darcy were offering his arm, Rebecca got to her feet. "No, don't disturb yourself, Mrs Daniels. I know where my coat is." She shook solemn hands with the card-players, all turning their cards face downwards, as she passed, she noticed, and escaped into the night.

He'd hardly recognised her, with her hair scraped back and that old-fashioned black dress. She looked like a caricature of a widow. Except, come to think of it, she looked merry enough, her eyes gleaming and her lips trying hard not to smile openly.

"Enjoyed yourself, did you?" he asked casually, as they left the pool of light provided by the security light over the front door.

"Immensely. In my own quiet way. I wish," she added, "that someone had pointed out to me that the old gentleman I thought was the caretaker was in fact a senior member of staff."

70

"I bollocked him for having you on." To his own ears he sounded defensive.

"He was very apologetic."

They walked on in silence. He'd have liked to tell her he wouldn't have left her on her own, that there were other people to protect her from his father. But he couldn't. He was ruffled by the Sowerby business.

"The wind's changed direction," she said suddenly. "I can smell the sea!"

"There's a lot of it about."

"Yes, but all I've seen is rain. And when my sister-in-law drove me down, we came on the M5 — didn't touch the coast at all."

"So you haven't seen the moors either."

"Only from my window."

"Oh, you've got to get up there. Forget the sea. What's the seaside at this time of year? But you want to get up on to the tors. You can be free up there." He shut up abruptly. No point in getting emotional.

"I could be free as a bird," she agreed, tartly. "But since the buses only run when they think about it, and the trains not even then, there's no great likelihood of my getting up there. Sorry. Didn't mean to snap."

"He doesn't pay you much?"

She told him.

"Hang on. That's less than the minimum wage. A lot less."

"He throws in the cottage, of course," she said dryly.

"Too bloody right he does."

They were now leaving even the occasional lights of the top part of the school drive. The lower half, further from the school, was unlit. They walked in silence — he thought she was worried about losing her footing; he wondered how she'd react if he were to take her arm to steady her. While he was still debating, the first lights in the lane came into view. Her cottage was only a couple of hundred yards away now. Come on, he had to say something, or she'd think — well, he didn't know what she'd think.

"How on earth does Tim cope in a place like Low Ash?" she asked without warning.

"There's times I think I ought to tell his dad to pull him out. Find somewhere better. The trouble is, Owen lives just up the road and when he's home it's nice for Tim to be able to go back for the weekend. And for me. When I get invited."

"Which, I should imagine, is pretty often."

Taken aback, he said, "We're only mates. I'm not — we don't —"

"I can see you're mates. More like brothers, I'd have said. But it must be hard to maintain a friendship with a younger boy without — without people making unwarranted assumptions."

She'd chickened out as well.

"They did. In fact, I went and had it out with Owen. I'm not shagging your kid, that sort of thing. He seemed OK about it. Sort of, anyway." He laughed, harshly. "It's just there's something about Tim. Sort of innocent but not silly. We get on."

"You'd miss him if his dad did pull him out."

"Yep. And he'll miss me when — when I go to university." Would she notice the hesitation? Of course she would. The question was, would she say anything?

She didn't. She was digging in her handbag — for Christ's sake, why had no one ever told her bags like that were for old women! She should have a shoulder bag!

She was looking up at him now, her face pale in the starlight. And she was smiling. He leaned down . . .

"Look — d'you see that old dog fox," he hissed, pointing.

She wouldn't, of course. Because there was no fox there. It was just that — just that he'd only been about to kiss her, hadn't he?

CHAPTER
NINE

Rebecca had just set off back up the hill towards Low Ash when she heard a woman's voice. "Cooeee! Coooeee!" She turned. A plump young woman with a baby buggy and a toddler in tow was waving to her.

To her? It was no one she knew. But she walked back, breaking into a smile when she saw how friendly the woman looked.

"You must be Rebecca. I'm Tamsin. Tamsin Brown. And these are Jack and Rosie." Jack disappeared behind his mother. Rosie produced a gummy smile.

Rebecca dropped on her haunches. "Hello, Jack. Hello, Rosie." Rosie shook a wild fist, then shoved it into her mouth.

"Teething," Tamsin said, as Rebecca straightened. "Mrs Gaye was saying we'd got someone else young moved into the village. And she said I ought to meet you."

"Soon as I'm settled," Rebecca said, "you must come and have a cup of tea."

Tamsin pulled a face. "Sounds from Mrs Gaye as if that'll be forever. No, you come in to us. After school — why not? We'll go and make some cakes, won't we, Jack?"

Jack looked doubtful.

"Love to," Rebecca declared. "If you're sure —"

"Cottage next to the church," Tamsin said.

"Red door," Jack said.

Rebecca smiled. "Cottage next to the church. Red door. But now I must fly."

"Yes — it doesn't do to be late when Payne-in-the-Arse is around," Tamsin said. "Bye!"

Rebecca had turned to scamper. But not quickly enough to avoid hearing Jack's voice: "Is that another grandma, Mummy?"

She must pretend not to have heard, of course. Tamsin would no doubt be wishing the lane could open up.

It wasn't as if she wasn't inured to comments like that. But it was one thing to hear them from a spoilt and vicious old man, another from a little boy with no axe to grind.

No. She wouldn't cry. If she hadn't cried on her own for fifteen long years, she wasn't going to start now.

Not now.

It would have been nice to see the boys before the weekend, but, though she dawdled for some minutes after she should have left the library, neither appeared. What on earth had got into Tony last night? He'd suddenly announced he could see a fox, and then had bolted as if a hound from hell were after him. No doubt he was violating some late rule and didn't want to embarrass her by implying she'd got him into trouble. All that stuff about his relationship with Tim. Did he protest too much? On the whole, she thought not. But he hadn't mentioned any girlfriends, either — not that that proved anything, in a monastic set-up like Low Ash.

But, she told herself, pulling on her coat, she had something else to look forward to: Tamsin's family. Tamsin looked sparky and modern. She was just the person to advise on clothes. Not that it was a matter of untrammelled choice. Not when you depended on what other people had bought and cast off. If such things mattered, you were always a year behind fashion. No, it shouldn't matter. Not when you were thirty-five. And frumpy. Rupert had always ridiculed and humiliated her when she'd gone for anything trendy: it had been easier to give in, and go for something safe. Something invisible. Except that beside Tamsin, in her crimson tunic and black leggings, she'd felt all too visible.

Out the mouths of babes and sucklings. "Another granny." It still hurt, like a bruise you can't stop fingering.

The cakes weren't quite ready, so she helped Jack finish an eccentric construction in plastic bricks. And then she'd helped him put the rest away, before little Rosie, dumped on the floor, could put any in her mouth.

"Marvellous stuff, Duplo, isn't it?" Tamsin said, carrying in a tea tray and looking for somewhere to put it. Rebecca pulled magazines and newspapers into an unsteady pile at the corner of the dining table to make room. She'd never seen quite as many things on every single flat surface. She'd have lived on the leavings of their reading matter for a week. Tamsin grabbed the pile and bore it off to the kitchen. "Paperbank," she said, over her shoulder.

So Tamsin had herself taught a stint at Low Ash.

"A few years back, now. One of the old geezers had a heart attack. I filled in for a bit. Can't say I enjoyed it overmuch. I mean, you expect high things of private education, don't you, not like the state system. But the kids weren't very bright, and there was no encouragement to do well. Oh, plenty of penalties if you didn't. But there was no doubt in my mind — or in the boys' — which was more important, sport or study. I did the make-up for them for their play. Oh, *The Rivals* or something. Produced by this guy who'd never even been to a theatre, let alone seen a play. And his wife as Mrs Malaprop. I kept on thinking her tits were going to pop out of the corset!" She lifted Rosie off her lap and dumped her on the floor.

"The Cowleys?"

"That's right. I wonder what they're doing this year. Not *Othello*, I hope — don't fancy doing the make-up for that. They'll want you to get involved — want to be my assistant?"

Rebecca made a non-committal noise. Hmm, maybe she would like to get involved.

And then Rosie started to choke.

"Cake," said Jack, helpfully.

"My God, my God," Tamsin screamed, grabbing her mobile phone.

They didn't have that long! They didn't have time for her to dial 999, let alone wait for an ambulance to wend its way through those lanes.

Rebecca grabbed the baby. She sat down, putting her across her knees. What next? That's right. She slapped her gently on the back. Nothing. Harder. Then gobbets of cake — could you really choke on something that small? — flew out, and suddenly all was pandemonium, Tamsin screaming, Jack yelling in outrage, and someone grabbing the baby and throwing Rebecca against the wall.

And in the midst of it all, squalls from Rosie. Proving, at very least, that she could breathe again.

And then Tamsin was laughing and crying, in the arms of a tall man. The person who'd turned on Rebecca, of course. Jack decided to have a little howl, too, so Rebecca gathered him up. At the imminent risk of another attack, she thought.

But soon she was being introduced and apologised to. Will had had no idea what was going on, had he? So it was natural to assume this strange woman was doing something dreadful to his precious daughter. Everything was fine, now. How about a little drink to celebrate?

Except Jack had found his own way to celebrate. As the wet patch all over Rebecca's blouse and skirt proved. Revolted, and knowing the urine had soaked through her petticoat too, Rebecca assumed Tamsin would offer her a change of clothes. OK, Tamsin's clothes would go round her twice, but at least they'd be dry. But since it was decreed the whole family was off on what they called the Tesco-run, no one seemed to think it necessary.

She didn't even get the drink Will had suggested.

So now she had another set of clothes to wash and dry. What she'd have to do was gather the whole lot into a sack, and make sure she got a bus for Newton Abbot, where she'd be sure to find a laundrette. And she'd better do it soon. At this rate she wouldn't have enough clothes to last the weekend.

Right. That was tomorrow morning booked. Or it would have been, had it not been for a hand-written note through the front door. She didn't know the writing.

Dear Mrs Wildbore
Is it too much to ask you to attend the auditions for the new School Production? You might find it not unamusing.
D.G. Cowley

Heavens, did they all write as if they'd been reading too much Henry James? She dropped the note on the table. She sniffed. There was an unfamiliar smell coming from upstairs. Plaster? Wet plaster? She shot upstairs. What fresh disaster did she have to face? She found, not a disaster, but a water tank, which, when she touched it, was warm. There was a note on that, too.

Dear Rebecca (If that's all right.)

I found I had some time to spare. Sorry about the ugly wiring, which I will have to deal with. But I had to give you a new ring-main.

Best regards

George Gaye.

PS Something in the kitchen for you.

If she had rushed upstairs, she flew down.

Well, she might never had seen a washing-machine this old — a twin-tub, as it happened — but if George had given it to her, she'd bet her life it would work. She knew there were pegs and a line in the outhouse. She was in business!

CHAPTER
TEN

George Gaye had been as good as his word as far as the paint was concerned, too. When Becky had gone to peg out her washing in the outhouse, she'd found a very large tin of magnolia emulsion, a roller and tray, and a couple of paint brushes. He'd even left dust-sheets! This weekend's work, then. Another weekend she'd have to sort out the mess in here — a wicker basket for a cycle, old Kilner jars, a deck chair with the original striped canvas, some bamboo canes and goodness knew what else. Another weekend. When she had the time, the energy . . . In the meantime, she should just be grateful for the enormous kindness of the Gayes.

The following morning, another glorious, Technicolor morning, the last thing she wanted to do was go into school for the auditions. Especially as there was no part for which she could imagine wishing to read. But since Mr Cowley had been courteous enough to invite her, she'd better just show her face, even if she simply smiled and made her exit.

Mr Cowley's red silk handkerchief had a daytime equivalent in a paisley silk cravat. With his dapper blazer and flannels, he looked more to Rebecca as if he were about to board a fifties yacht, but he smiled with

81

apparent delight and quite understood — in her tragic circumstances (he dropped his voice and his eyes, as if encompassing the darkest widows' weeds) — her natural reluctance to tread the boards.

"But my dear Mrs Wildbore — or may I call you Rebecca? — I do hope I might prevail on you to play some part in our endeavour. Someone to assist me . . . to prompt at early rehearsals? There! I can see an answering gleam in your eyes!"

Could he? And whoever heard of a prompter in only the early stages of a production? But somehow, yes, she heard herself agreeing.

Escaping, she was just going into the village shop to thank the Gayes, when a bus drew up, with Exeter on the front sign board. On impulse she joined the little queue and jumped on. What if she could find some cheap curtains? Oh, it would be grand to make her own, but that would mean — no, she couldn't face finding someone with a machine to lend her, and even she wasn't crazy enough to think of running them up by hand!

She was too busy trying to see the countryside to bother about her fellow-passengers. But the bus was going through rich farming land, not the wide-open moorland she craved. Better than an industrial city, though, she told herself irritably. Enough of this self-pity. She might not be young any more, but she was alive. And with life, as the cliché went, came hope.

But hope could evaporate, too. And it evaporated steadily as she trudged through Exeter hunting for ready-made curtains even approximately in her price range. There was no point in looking at clothes. Not with her budget. Not even charity shop clothes, not if she had to buy curtains.

She'd better go home. Except the return bus wouldn't go for another hour yet. And some puritan part of her — no, some residue of Rupert! — resented paying the bus-fare and buying nothing at all.

Well, she could buy some wellies and gardening gloves. Easy. The gardening gloves were even on special offer. She thought of buying some cheap garden tools but rejected them as too flimsy for her wilderness.

"Mrs Wildbore! Mrs Wildbore! Rebecca!"

Someone calling her? In Exeter? She turned, to see Mrs Cowley waving frantically at her, and managing a little wobbly jog to catch up.

"There! I knew it was you. How are you, my dear? Busy, I should think. Those boys keep you on your toes, don't they? Now, what have you been buying?" Mrs Cowley peered in vain for bulging carrier bags from fashionable stores to match her own. Her face fell. "Oh dear, how very sensible."

Rebecca tried not to smile. "I was hoping to get some curtains."

"Oh, not here. I know just the place. Newton Abbot. Not far from the race-course. You want to try there."

Rebecca nodded. Want she might. But how could she get to Newton?

"Now, I need a nice cup of tea, and I know a place where they do these wicked little cakes. Come on."

Rebecca shook her head. "I'm on the bus. And I don't even know exactly where it goes from."

"Bus? Dear Clifford would never forgive me if I let you go on the bus! Not when I have my little car here. Oh, do come and have a coffee. My treat! My shopping's never complete without one of those cakes. And you can tell me why you've been so very naughty and not gone to the auditions."

Rebecca laughed. "The same might be said of you, surely, Mrs Cowley?"

"Isobel. Oh, I'm too old, my dear. And dear Desmond would really like to do an all-male production. Though where he'll find anyone in those boys to take on Gertrude, I don't know."

Rebecca fell into step as Isobel turned purposefully towards a tea-shop. "Gertrude? They're doing *Hamlet*!"

"To be honest, my dear, dear Desmond and I do feel that it's a wee bit beyond this intake of boys. But there — once Clifford gets the bit between his teeth, there really is no stopping him. And of course, young Antony will be so good as Hamlet. And Curtis — I can just see him as Laertes."

Nothing like a bit of type-casting! Or situation-casting. And it seemed as if she'd fallen into Dear Desmond's nicely sprung trap. No, of course he'd never wanted her to act. He'd wanted her as prompter all along.

She'd have been much safer on the bus. She'd known that from the minute Isobel Cowley had pulled her

84

mini out of the parking-slot in the multi-storey car-park.

Some people can talk and drive. Others — particularly those who need their hands as much as their mouths — can't. Isobel couldn't. Pillars leapt at the car from nowhere, other cars materialised at random. And they hadn't reached the street, yet.

How they got as far as the trunk road to take them south and west without hitting anything, Rebecca had no idea. Was it best to talk herself, although Isobel liked to look at her, or to let Isobel do all the talking, complete with gestures when both hands ought to have been firmly on the wheel?

At least Isobel didn't have enough ambition or the mini didn't have enough power to overtake on the long hill out of Exeter. But sooner or later they'd be off the dual carriageway and on to narrow country roads. Rebecca had never been sick with fear before.

The inevitable happened at an island, just as they were leaving the main road. Isobel clearly had no concept of giving way to the right. Or indeed, of giving way full-stop. And there was a Volvo coming round fast. No faster than he was entitled to be. But fast. And out pulled Isobel, hands and tongue flapping, straight into his path.

Close your eyes. Cover your face. Brace yourself.

Wait for the impact.

Which came. But almost tenderly.

The Volvo driver had wrenched his car — it had been his tyres screaming, not Isobel's — so that he ended half on the island itself. And by a miracle the bumpers had done no more than touch.

Rebecca was out of the car before she knew what she was doing.

Isobel followed. "Now, young man, what *do* you think you are doing? This is a public road."

The other driver emerged, white; Rebecca could see him shaking. Rebecca stood rooted. Those eyes. That face. His face was so familiar. Was he on TV or something? No: if she'd ever seen the chiselled features, the fine skin and those deep blue eyes, surely she'd never have forgotten them.

"Owen! I didn't know you were back with us!" Isobel contrived to change sentences much more smoothly than she'd managed her gear changes. "You've been away again?"

The poor man nodded. And managed a smile of icy courtesy. Even his teeth were good. He couldn't be more than forty — possibly not much more than Rebecca herself. And he was as trim as a boy.

"Where have you been this time?" Isobel demanded.

"The States," he said, in a voice that could have read telephone directories and still kept her interest.

"Ah, so you're jet-lagged, you poor man. Now you get home to bed. I was going to say, fast as you can!" Isobel giggled. "Slowly and safely, that's what I mean. Off you go."

You meet a man like that once in a lifetime, and you meet him when a chance acquaintance has run him off the road and then slandered him. Rebecca couldn't have mistaken the contempt for Isobel in his eyes.

Contempt which had no doubt included her — had he even noticed her. And she was by no means certain she'd have wanted him to. Looking like this? Her hair — did she ever have good hair days? And in this outfit even she had considered too shabby for school and had only put on this morning because everything else was still drying?

"I'm afraid," he said, still courteously, "I can't move until you have."

"Oh, silly me. Now, you look after yourself, Owen dear, and no more little mistakes. We won't say anything, will we, dear?"

So now he had to look at her!

"Not a word," Rebecca said, praying he would pick up her irony. She had to distance herself from Isobel, just in case they should ever meet again. Except that was being disloyal to someone trying to be kind. Hell and hell and hell!

"Such a nice young man," Isobel declared, cajoling then forcing the car into reverse. "Always the gentleman. Though the same can't be said for some of his friends, it has to be said." She twiddled her fingers in a friendly wave as she pulled away, failing to worry about a container lorry approaching.

"Did you call him Owen?" Rebecca managed, as the sound of the lorry's horn faded.

"Yes. Owen Griffiths."

Of course! Tim's father! Though she couldn't imagine Tim's gentle features ever shifting into those forbidding planes.

"His son's at the school. Nice boy. But a bit too close to Tony for Clifford's liking — you know, these pretty boys and their insinuating little ways."

How dared she impugn Tim? Or Tony, for that matter. "I don't," she said flatly. "And I am absolutely certain that Tim and Tony are no more than friends. And no less than friends."

"Really, my dear, there's no need to take that tone. Still, I suppose you were upset by Owen — not very apologetic, was he?"

Rebecca shook her head.

"There are some people who consider him quite nice looking — the father, I mean."

Nice looking! He was simply the most handsome man she'd ever seen.

"And, of course, he's got a nice voice — he takes solos in the church choir, when he can be bothered, that is. Not that he graces us with his presence all that often. These jet-setters."

Rebecca had never given the matter much thought, but she wouldn't have associated jet-setters with Volvos. Or with small Devon villages or with fourth-rate boarding schools.

Though she thanked Isobel profusely, Rebecca wondered if her legs would ever stop shaking. She told herself firmly that a strong sweet cup of tea would calm her down. But that would have to wait. What on earth was sitting on her doorstep?

Very gingerly, she opened the carrier bag. The smell of wet and rotting onions jumped out at her. She closed it again. There was a note attached to it.

A little thank-you for your quick-thinking last night!
Love
Tamsin
XXX

Holding her breath, she peered in. The bag was full not of onions but of shallots. Some were already fit for nothing but a compost heap — she could add them to the one she started during her garden-tidying. The rest needed immediate attention — soaking in brine overnight and then bottling in vinegar.

Well, in the out-house, she had more than enough jars. But she didn't have nearly enough salt, or any vinegar. She glanced at her watch. Five twenty-two. If she ran, she might just make it to the village shop.

Mrs Gaye was just turning the sign from OPEN to CLOSED, but she smiled and pulled back the bolts.

"I thought you'd be down for your bread, my dear, but now I find Trish has been and sold it."

Bread! She'd forgotten all about it!

"But I've got a granary in my freezer if you wouldn't mind that."

"Mind! You've saved my life! But I need other things, and I'm taking up your time."

"Never you mind about that, my dear. It's good to have someone doing her shopping with us, instead of the supermarkets. Salt . . . Vinegar . . . You'll be doing a bit of pickling, then?" Unasked she produced a packet of pickling spices. "On top of all the other things you've got to do?"

"Well, Tamsin — I don't remember her other name — gave me some shallots."

"Tamsin Brown. Lives by the church." Mrs Gaye did not sound particularly enthusiastic.

"That's right. The most delightful little boy. And a baby girl."

"Hmm. Now, anything else? Do you want me to put aside a paper for you tomorrow?"

Oh, the luxury of a Sunday newspaper! Rupert had axed those years ago.

"Yes, please," she said, picking up her groceries absently. What could she cut down on to pay for the paper?

What the — ? She was treading hard on someone's foot. Who else's, but Owen Griffiths'? Even in the late dusk, it was too much to hope he wouldn't recognise her.

Like a teenager tripping over a pop-star, she babbled her apologies and bolted.

It was only as she got halfway up the lane she realised she'd never asked Mrs Gaye to pass on her thanks to George. Well, all she had to do was did as he did — write a little note. But she'd make sure that Owen Griffiths was well clear of the shop before she tried to deliver it.

CHAPTER
ELEVEN

Owen watched the boys file into church. He wasn't at all sure about this sort of enforced religion, but if the boys hadn't had to come every week, the vicar wouldn't have been able to justify a weekly service in the village church. When the school holidays came round, there was never more than a handful listening to Mike Green's sensible sermons.

Owen knew better than to try and catch Tim's eye, any more than he would try and hug him after the service. The trouble was that these days Tim's hugs had to be spontaneous, like one footballer celebrating another's goal. Growing up. That was the problem. So who was Tim grinning at, briefly and illicitly, from his seat in the choir? Without the crassest of head-twisting, there was no way he'd see. Still, maybe Tim would introduce him to whoever it was after the service.

But after the service Tim was peering round the churchyard looking for someone. So hard he missed Owen's wave. But at last he managed to catch his son's eye, and Tim bounded over. From the far side of a tombstone, Tony flapped a lazy hand, but made no effort to join them. Yes, he had more tact than his father, who was bustling over purposefully until intercepted by Mike Green. And even Clifford-Payne stopped for clergymen.

"Hi," was all the greeting he got. But it would do, and the two headed for the car.

"Did you get those CDs, Dad?"

"I did. And did you get the part?"

"I did." He stopped long enough to produce an extravagant bow. "And I vow 'tis well deserved. Tell you what, though — casting Curtis —"

"Not as Hamlet!"

"No. Laertes. Tony's Hamlet, of course. But it won't half add to — to —"

"The verisimilitude?"

"That's right. Yes, I got an A for the last English assignment and two red ticks by that word. All I've got to do now is remember it. And remember how to spell it." He looked round.

"So which part did you get?"

"Oh. Osric." He was peering round again.

"Looking for anyone special?" Owen asked.

"Sort of. No, she's gone."

She! Tim was certainly growing up. What did he dare ask? "Were you expecting to see her?" he tried.

"Well, she was in church all right. Must have pushed off home, I suppose . . ."

"Home? Does she live round here?" How on earth had Tim met a girl? Round here? In term-time, when almost every waking moment was supervised? Unless Clifford-Payne had at last got sane and started making contacts with local schools.

"Yes, that old cottage that the poet squatted in. Near the school gates. You remember, we saw signs of life last week."

Did they? Somehow last Sunday seemed a long time ago. At least he'd come back with a good contract under his belt.

"What's for lunch?"

"Well, you can choose. There's the Stag's Head, or I've got some steak, some mushrooms and a few potatoes."

"Enough for chips?"

"Enough for chips."

They were driving up to Penkridge House when Tim started again.

"I can't understand it. She's usually so friendly. Mind you, she's very shy. And she must have an awful lot to do at that cottage."

This didn't sound like your average teenage girl.

"Is she with her parents?"

"No! For goodness' sake, Dad, she's too old for parents. Well, you know what I mean."

Owen didn't, but wasn't about to admit it. "Does she have a name?"

"We're supposed to call her Mrs Wildbore but Tony and I call her Rebecca. Well, Tony does. I tend to call her Mrs W. She's the new librarian."

"Ah! Mrs Cowley's replacement." Was Tim busy developing a crush? That was a new development.

"Yes. But better than Ma Cowley. And nicer. When you get to know her."

"And until you get to know her she's a real dragon?"

Tim laughed, patronisingly. "You know, Dad, we were doing stereotypes the other day. And I think you've got some sort of stereotype librarian in your head."

Taken aback, Owen said, "Plain, thick glasses, no sense of humour —"

"Tut, tut. Well, she does seem plain, but . . . No specs, anyway. These awful clothes. And I wish she'd get that hair of hers sorted. But — well, she stopped me and Tony copping it from the Swine. And she's got a sense of humour. And she's sort of brave, too. Which I suppose she'd have to be, if she's going to marry old Payne-in-the-Arse."

"Is she, by Christ?"

"Tony thinks so. Mind you, he's going to try and stop it."

"Selfish little bastard!" It was out before he knew. "It doesn't matter whether he likes the woman, so long as his father does."

Tim looked at him reproachfully. "That's not what you've always said to me when you've brought one of your women along. Anyway, you've got it quite wrong. Tony wants to break it up not because he doesn't like her, but because he does. And not, before you ask, in that way. They're sort of mates. Like Tony and I are."

Owen's brain was working overtime. "Hang on. Remember I'm jet-lagged. Let me just run through this again. There's this plainish middle-aged woman who's working at the school and Tony wants to get her out of the Chief's clutches."

"Right."

Jet-lagged. The word recalled a couple of yesterday's events. "Hair all nohow? Jumble sale clothes? I suppose she isn't about five three?"

"Yes! That's right. How do you know?"

"I saw her a couple of times yesterday. You know, around the village." This was not the time to favour Tim with a succinct account of what he thought of Mrs Whatever-her-name-was's manners. Not to mention her taste in friends. No doubt the presence of a woman was stirring a few hormones. Tim's and half the school's. But everything would soon settle down. It usually did. He pointed to a sad heap at the edge of the lane. "I do wish old Brock would take more care crossing the road . . ."

More at a loose end without Tim than he cared to admit, Tony decided to take himself for a run. Rebecca was probably feeling a bit low, too, being a widow on her own, so he might drop by for a cup of tea. Why had she scuttled off after church so fast? Silly cow. Church was a good place to meet people. Real people, not just Low Ash people. Mind you, she'd looked a bit upset — yes, a bit embarrassed or upset or something.

And if she'd looked a bit upset this morning, what about now? He stared down at her as she opened the front door, her face running with tears.

But she was trying to smile. "It's the shallots, Tony. I'm busy peeling shallots. Come on through — if you can stand the smell."

Smell! The kitchen bloody stank! She'd got a bucket of muddy water, with some orange things lurking in the murk, a colander full of peeled shallots, and, on a piece of soaked newspaper, a pile of fine orange shallot skins.

He looked at her hands. "You should be wearing rubber gloves."

"I know. But I forgot until the Gayes were shut."

"They wouldn't have minded your knocking on their door. Folk are always doing it."

"They've done so much for me, I couldn't put them to any more trouble." She looked as if she were going to explain but she turned abruptly. "I suppose if you're running you shouldn't have a cup of tea?"

She looked as if she needed one, even if they were nothing more than onion tears. "Go on, one won't kill me. I'll put the kettle on, shall I? Hey, what's this camping stove doing here?"

"Supplementing the stove. It's kaput."

"You need to get —"

"— the bursar on to that!"

Her whole face changed when she laughed, didn't it?

"Did I hear some music when I came past?"

She jerked her head at a tiny transistor radio. The sort you could get for less than twenty quid. "Reception's pretty poor round here, though."

He picked it up. "Maybe you need to retune it?"

"Be my guest."

He did his best, but there were still too many whistles and clicks for Radio Three to be any good. "D'you play at all?"

"Used to. Not any more." That put the full-stop on that, didn't it? What had he said to upset her? Whatever it was, he was out of his depth. He'd better try something else.

"I got Hamlet yesterday."

"Did you? Oh, that's brilliant." He thought for a moment that she was going to give him a dramatic hug, the sort you give a bloke who'd just scored a try. But she put her arms down again, and said, "And who's your Horatio? And Laertes? No, don't tell me they've got Curtis as Laertes! Now, that could be interesting . . ."

"Yeah. Could be, couldn't it?"

He'd left soon after that. He had that essay to finish after all. And he had, as he looked round that tip of a cottage, the strongest feeling that it wasn't just the shallots that were making her cry.

No cello or bass guitar this time: Tim had left them at the school since his exeat was for such a short time. Owen sensed that Clifford-Payne had been awkward about the day's leave, though he didn't think he'd get to the bottom of it with Tim in his present mood. He'd been quiet all afternoon and, though he had once or twice seemed on the verge of speaking, he'd always clammed up as soon as Owen took an interest. Not that Owen was at his best either. He *had* been jet-lagged when he'd nearly hit that Cowley woman. He shouldn't really have been driving in that state. And it had really been his fault, that librarian woman stamping on his foot. He could see she was coming out of the shop and should have noticed the daze she was in. And it had earned him, no doubt about it, a black mark from Mary Gaye.

"If I could get you an evening's exeat some night during the week, would you fancy coming bowling or something?" he asked, as if that could undo some of his mistakes. "No?"

"Love to. But Payne-in-the-Arse is being dead tricky at the moment. And you never know when I'll be desperate to get out. Anyway, you've got that score to sort out. Let's leave it till things are —" He stopped, abruptly.

What on earth had he been going to say?

"You sure things are OK, Tim? You would tell me if things were bad?"

"Sure."

"You promise?"

"OK, Dad," Tim conceded, sighing hugely, "I promise. Oh, I nearly forgot. There's a note from P.A. It's in the hall. On the table."

They drove in silence the last few hundred yards. But Owen had a distinct impression of Tim staring hard out of the window as they drove past the librarian's cottage.

CHAPTER
TWELVE

"Now, my dear Mrs Wildbore," Sowerby began, in a close parody of Clifford, "I have two suggestions to make about the disposal of your time this morning. But first I would like to apologise for the rudeness of myself, my fellow guests and indeed our host the other night. Playing bridge and thus excluding you. Indeed, I would never have countenanced it, had I not had the distinct impression that you found the whole experience more amusing, the worse it became. Deny it if you can!" he concluded, twinkling benignly.

Rebecca laughed. "I was taught never to tell lies, Mr Sowerby!" So why, all the last years, had she lived a lie?

"Quite right. Now, what I suspect, and you are in no position even to guess, is that the worst malefactors in this book business are not the boys, reprobates though they certainly are. No, the worst hoarders are my colleagues. I suggest you close the library at ten — a quiet time, if my memory serves me right — and pay us a visit in the staff room. The experience may not be pleasant, but it will certainly be educational. Till ten, then, Mrs Wildbore!"

She held up a finger. "You said you had two experiences in mind, Mr Sowerby!"

"So I did. What a memory!" His eyes shone with intelligence — how could she ever have thought he was a caretaker! "Well, I believe it is the custom in co-educational establishments for assignations to be arranged for behind the cycle sheds. I would like to propose an assignation, Mrs Wildbore, at the cycle sheds. In front of them, I think. At twelve fifteen — which is, I think, the time at which you are supposed to close the library. Not twelve thirty. You should not be working without pay."

"It's the time when the boys like to use it —"

"In that case . . . No, let me think about this. There is more than one way of skinning a cat. Till ten, then, Mrs Wildbore."

At ten sharp, Rebecca presented herself, with a black bin-liner for the books, outside the staff room. To knock or not to knock? She was pretty sure the masters would expect her to tap and wait. On the other hand, she was supposed to be a colleague, not just some hired help. She'd just decided to knock and go in when Cavendish sailed up, that dreadful gown in mid-billow. Seeing her seemed to take the wind out of it, however.

"Mrs Wildbore? What on earth are you doing here?"

From his tone he might have come across her in the male loo.

"She's here to retrieve library books, Cavendish." Sowerby came up behind them. "Do come in, Mrs Wildbore." He opened the door and ushered her through first.

He had, of course, intended to create a stir, and he succeeded admirably. Faces changed — in the space of a second — from apoplectic with rage at the presence of an unaccompanied woman to apologetic when they saw who did in fact accompany her. Embarrassed though she certainly was, she couldn't help but be amused. And furious, that someone like Swain should take one look at her and throw down his paper, storming out of the room with a vicious slam of the door. She thought she caught the words, "filthy creature," but couldn't be sure.

She looked around her. The chairs weren't in much better condition than those at her cottage, and the carpet, though new, was already grey with cigarette ash. What century were these people living in? Hadn't they heard of the dangers of smoking? Of passive smoking? And what about simple things like regular cleaning? Or perhaps the few cleaners she saw about the place were — as women — banned from the place. So why didn't the caretaker — the real one — take responsibility for it?

Sowerby took in her expression and raised an eyebrow. "I see you've brought with you a bin-liner, Mrs Wildbore. I'm afraid many of the items here are no better worth."

She set briskly about the task, anxious to escape the foul atmosphere as quickly as possible. Within five minutes her sack was almost too heavy to carry. She could see what looked suspiciously like more of her quarry high on a set of bookshelves. To reach them she'd need a ladder. And jeans, given the present company.

She collected together a small pile from the window-sill — when had the windows last met a window-cleaner? She couldn't carry them in the bin-liner, so she stacked them neatly by the door.

"I'll come back for them in a few minutes," she told Sowerby, picking up the polythene sack.

"It would be nice to think that one of my colleagues would be chivalrous enough to carry them for you," he observed, taking it from her. "Allow me, Mrs Wildbore."

There was a stunned silence.

In response she gathered the pile up herself and left the room.

She was only two strides down the corridor when she heard the door open and close. Not that she would turn back.

"Mrs Wildbore! Rebecca!"

Cavendish! She slowed, half-turning, but did not halt. Sowerby was striding ahead, as much as he could stride, with a stoop like that.

"Please — allow me!" He reached for the armful of books.

She smiled, but shook her head. "I'm already filthy, Mr Cavendish," she said with no particular emphasis.

He gestured — his gown was shabby enough. "Jeremy," he said.

"And if you try and take any I shall probably drop the lot."

"And when they hit the floor we shall all die of asphyxiation. You know," he said, falling into step with her, "it isn't until you see something familiar through someone else's eyes that you really see it. That room, for instance. That really is 'filthy'."

She glanced at him sharply: was he picking up her adjective or Swain's?

"It was dirty when I joined," he continued without hesitation. "I suppose it might have had a bit of a clean-up when they laid the new carpet. And I know there was a bit of a row. The maintenance man wanted to slosh some emulsion over the walls. But — there was opposition."

Rebecca could imagine George's exasperation. He was the sort of man who'd want to see a job well done.

"Look," Cavendish pursued, "if you're on your own, Rebecca, would you fancy coming out for a jar some time? You know, just a quiet drink? Whoops!"

Once the books had started to cascade there was no stopping them. Cavendish tried to help, but jumped back from the clouds of dust. At last, peering at the few she still clutched, he pointed. "Oh, let them go too. It'll save you a job! I know you've been dusting the others as you put them back — you won't have to take a duster to these."

She obliged. Their laughter rang along the corridor.

At last, he sank with some grace to one knee. After a moment's thought, she stayed upright, holding her arms for the first stack of books. He collected the rest into a similar tower for himself and they set off.

The black sack was sitting by her desk, but there was no sign of Sowerby.

He was prompt to the minute, however, for their cycle shed assignation. An unmistakable shape was inadequately concealed by his gown, which he whisked away and put back on as she approached.

"Hey presto! Your transport, my dear."

"Transport of delight!" she exclaimed. "Oh, Mr Sowerby, how splendid."

"I don't think you'll find it all that splendid. It can't be less than forty years old. But it's in good condition, as you can see. Perfectly sound mechanically — I asked the inestimable George to check such matters as brakes."

"I'd love to try it."

"Suit the deed to the word."

She did. At first she wobbled but as soon as she realised that the worst she could do was fall off, she started to trundle along. "I've not been on a bike since I left home — eighteen, I'd be." Sowerby stood, arms akimbo, watching her.

She was so exhilarated that she waved to Clifford as he hove into view.

"Look what Mr Sowerby's been kind enough to lend me," she called. She circled widely round him, and came to a halt not far from Mr Sowerby.

"The verb is 'to give'," he said quietly. "A worthy performance, my dear," he said out loud.

"But not one, if you will permit me to observe, that should be repeated in the school grounds," Clifford said.

She stared. "All the boys have bikes."

"They, Mrs Wildbore, are boys. Wearing trousers."

"Well, I shall wear my jeans when I ride it. I shall need jeans to venture into that staff room again. It's disgusting!"

"The staff room!"

"Mrs Wildbore was collecting stray books, Payne," Sowerby said sharply.

"Ladies on my staff do not wear trousers of any kind. And you can send one of the older boys to collect the rest of the books. Sowerby, a word in your ear, if you please."

Sowerby produced an extravagant wink from the eye further from Clifford, and a tiny flap of the hand. Rebecca was to take herself off. She thought for a moment of staying and defending the old man. But either he could defend himself better without her, or he might prefer to be rebuked without an audience.

Despite the offending — and confining — skirt, she sang aloud as she bowled down the hill.

"Do you think I'll ever be able to make my legs walk again?" she demanded as Sowerby came to return the *Guardian* the following morning. He took no notice of the injunction she regularly stamped on all the papers. Nor did she expect him to. She did rather wish, however, he didn't complete the crossword with quite such humiliating speed. But presumably the rest of the staff were equally humiliated. "Every muscle's screaming."

"Wait till you've tried some of our real hills," he said.

Cavendish appeared. "Morning, Sowerby. Rebecca."

She nodded. "Mr Cavendish. Jeremy."

"I hear you've got a bike."

"Thanks to Mr Sowerby," she said, smiling at the older man.

"I must dig out my mountain bike," Cavendish said. "We could go on a few rides, couldn't we?" He smiled and was gone.

"Did you ever study Latin, my dear?" Sowerby asked.

"Latin A Level."

"I thought as much. Do you remember the different ways you can ask a question in Latin?"

She shook her head. "Barely."

He twinkled a disbelieving eye. "Well, there are some open questions — you can answer how you please. But there are other questions —"

"— which expect you to answer yes or no!"

"Exactly. Now, when Cavendish phrased that question, did he expect you to answer yes or no?"

"Yes, I rather think."

"And I wonder whether you will." He turned his back and shuffled away before she could answer.

CHAPTER
THIRTEEN

The music in Owen's head almost hurt him with the pressure to be written down before it evaporated. It wasn't often it came like this, so when it did, he had to obey it. Thank goodness for computer programs — he couldn't bear to have to scrawl all this down only to find he couldn't decipher his handwriting.

At last he realised his back was aching, and a familiar throb was starting in his right elbow. Time to stop, then, for a break. Hell. Two fifteen already! He'd been working since eight. No wonder his body was protesting.

He stretched, going through the routine designed to unlock stiff joints and relax tired tendons. He couldn't afford to be laid up now, couldn't afford another dose of that wretched tennis elbow. Lose a few minutes to gain a few minutes — that was the way to look at it.

What was in the fridge? Salad? Bread? Cheese?

The phone rang.

Let it ring. The answerphone could take it, as it had taken half a dozen other calls this morning. He'd deal with all that stuff this evening.

But there was something about the voice that made him push open the kitchen door a little further. And something in the words that took him across the hall in two strides.

"Mr Griffiths? If you are there, pick up the phone. Please. There's been an accident, you see —"

He snatched the receiver. "Griffiths here. What's going on?"

"Your son's ill. He's at my cottage — the one near the school gate. It looks as if he's had a bang on the head. An ambulance is on its way. But I thought you'd want to know — oh, he's going to be sick again —" The line went dead.

Jesus! This was what he'd always dreaded. Grabbing coat and keys, he sprinted to the car, dashing away tears. He'd got to reverse the damned thing. Why hadn't he put it in backwards, why hadn't he had the drive straightened, why . . .

Why was Tim at that cottage? It didn't make sense.

He forced himself to slow as he came to the sharp corner. Once round that he could at least start driving forwards. If not in a straight line.

He took deep breaths. Smashing the car wouldn't help Tim — into a tree or into Ma Cowley, puttering along at twenty in the middle of the bloody road. No good flashing her. If she did see him in the mirror — pretty unlikely — she'd simply wave back. He must tell Tim — tell Tim . . .

An accident. A bang on the head. It didn't make sense.

Why at that woman's cottage?

At last the Cowley woman pulled off. He floored the accelerator, only having to brake again to take an awkward bend. Sodding Devon lanes!

At last. He flung the car on to the grass verge and sprinted to the cottage.

The front door was wide open.

"Come along in," a woman's voice called.

He obeyed. He stopped long enough to take in the scene. Tim was lying on the floor. Ashen-white, he was vomiting into a red plastic bowl. The woman, applying what must be cold cloths to his forehead, took the bowl gently away.

"Here's your dad, Tim, love," she said.

Tim muttered something and clutched her hand convulsively.

My God, my God.

She looked up at Owen: "He keeps drifting in and out of consciousness. That sounds like the paramedics now."

He listened. Yes, at last he picked up the sound of the siren. It was a long way away yet.

"Can you take his hand — I'll empty this."

But Tim clutched her again. Owen grabbed the bowl, found the bathroom, emptied it.

"Thanks. Now, can you throw a bowl of water on the bonfire? I think it's out, but best make sure."

Bonfire? Why was she playing at bonfires when Tim was like that? But he did as he was told. She'd already scattered the embers. Something wrapped in kitchen foil gleamed amongst them. He slung the water.

"Thanks. Just go and make sure they know this is the place, will you?"

He dashed outside, waving both arms. The ambulance was already parked, its back-door open. So why . . . ?

Tim had vomited again. Without speaking he picked up the bowl. Emptied it, like an automaton. Still, she knelt there.

"Could you lock the back door for me? And shut the windows?" What the hell was she doing, ordering him about like this when Tim might be dying? Might be dying . . .

When he hurtled downstairs at last, she smiled, as if that would reassure him. "They think it's just concussion. But they're getting him into hospital." Is that what she'd wanted? To have him out of the way while they examined him?

Was it minutes or hours before they started to move Tim? But at last, his hand still clamped to the woman's, they lifted him. And she fell face down. What the hell was she doing?

"Legs gone to sleep, my dear? You been like that long enough for them to drop off," one of the paramedics said.

She smiled as his colleague fielded her. He looked to Owen to help him.

Still Tim hung on.

"You'll be coming with us in the ambulance, then?"

"Of course," Owen said.

"I meant his mum, Sir. You'll both be needing to get back somehow — won't you be following in your car?"

"She's not — I'm . . . Sorry, of course I'll follow." What did he mean, wanting to get back? When?

The woman said, "They'll be wanting to keep him in, I dare say. Just to keep an eye on him. And you'll want to come home."

110

Owen shook his head — none of this made sense. "You mean —"

"Looks like just a sharp bit of concussion, nothing serious," the first man said. "But with head injuries it's always best to make sure. Hang on there, old chap."

But Tim had started to vomit again. Some missed the bowl. She didn't seem to turn a hair.

She handed him her keys. Locking a dump like this! There was nothing in there a burglar would want. And surely — he took one last glance at the bonfire — it would be better burned down.

But not with his son in it.

There was no way he could keep up with the ambulance, and after a while he told himself he was crazy to try. Tim wouldn't know he was there fifty or five hundred yards away. The vital thing was simply to get there.

He didn't know he was crying till the tears dropped on to his jeans.

By the time he'd found a parking slot and — yes, they wanted fifty pence for a ticket! — he could hardly walk. But he ran, all the way, desperate to find A&E. Tim was nowhere to be seen.

"It's good news," a voice was saying. "Mr Griffiths — can you understand? It's good news!"

He looked down. It was the woman. She put her hand on his arm. "He came round for a few minutes. He's going to be fine."

He shook her off. "Fine! What do you know about fine?"

"They'll keep him in, of course, and do a brain scan just to make sure. But I promise you, he opened his eyes and this time he could focus and he asked where you were. Come and sit down. They'll take you in in a few minutes. Oh, and you'll need to register him and everything."

"He asked for me?"

She laughed. What was she doing, laughing? "You make it sound like some deathbed request."

He stabbed a finger at her chest. "You don't know what it is to have a child —"

"No."

Even he heard the pain in her voice. What was he doing, lashing out like that? When he ought to be grateful to her? He sought for words to frame an apology. Found none that were adequate.

She said, "Mr Griffiths, Tim said, 'I thought I heard Dad. Where is he?' And when I said you were following, he said that that would teach you to buy a dowager's car. And he smiled. Come on, sit down. You look as if you could use a coffee."

He looked at her, seeing her for the first time. He managed a smile. "So do you."

"I forgot to ask you to bring my bag —"

"I used all my change for parking." He was ready to laugh. Or cry. "A brain scan!"

"Routine. But if there were any blood-clots, they'd be able to pinpoint them and remove them."

"Mr Griffiths? Mr Griffiths?" It took moments to realise it was him the nurse was calling.

The woman pushed him gently: "Go on."

If she didn't eat or drink something soon, she would faint. She knew she would. And she knew Owen Griffiths should eat, too. Short of robbing a Hospital Friends' collection box, however, what could she do? Without her bag, she was penniless. And that meant she was dependent on him either for a lift home or for bus fare.

Not that she could blame him. Bags probably hadn't been uppermost in the poor man's mind at the time.

He'd been gone a long time. A long time. God, what if there were a problem? What if Tim were worse than they'd said? Oh, God. No tissues. In her bag, of course. And the hand she smudged her tears away with smelt of Tim's vomit.

There was a lavatory over there. But she didn't even go that far, just in case. Just in case what? In case Owen should need her to comfort him? In which case he'd look for her, wait till she reappeared. Or in case he simply forgot about her. Which was she really afraid of?

"Rebecca?"

She jumped.

He sat down beside her. "He's still conscious — but he's got a cracking headache and he's hardly arguing about staying in. I said I'd stay all night if he wanted, but he said not. They've got to put him in an adult ward, so he's got to be grown up."

"No mercy dash for his favourite teddy bear, then?"

"Not if we want to live." He smiled. "You really look as if you could use a coffee. There's a little cafeteria place over there. They'll call us there when they want us."

"I need to wash my hands first." She held them up. "I was in the garden when I heard something — I'd been having a bonfire, you see, and I wanted to bring those dead heads through from the front garden. And I heard this moan —"

"Tim?"

She nodded. "Sort of drunk, he looked. Staggering along the road. And then he collapsed."

"How on earth did you get him inside?" Tim was nearly as tall as she, and possibly heavier.

"I managed. Oh, dear. Hell," she caught herself up short. "I don't have so much as a tissue." She sniffed, pressing the back of her hand to her mouth.

He patted his pockets. "Neither have I! Look, let's go on a raiding party to the loos — paper towels or toilet roll — and we'll go and have a coffee and a damned good cry."

For all he was grown-up enough to be in an adult ward, Tim held open his arms like a child. Owen hung back, until she pushed him forward. It wasn't many men who were privileged to hug their teenage sons — let him enjoy it while he had the excuse. And then, turning his face from her in embarrassment, Owen scrambled to his feet to make way for her.

"I thought I smelt baked potatoes," Tim said, after giving her a more perfunctory hug. "I'm sure I did."

"You probably did. On my bonfire."

Owen stopped to stare at her as they left the ward. "That was your lunch I threw the water over. Why didn't you tell me you hadn't eaten?"

"Have you?"

He shook his head and fell into step with her. "We'd better eat, then. Properly."

This time it was she who stopped. "I'm not really dressed to eat anywhere proper."

"For God's sake, woman —" He meant to laugh her out of her coyness. But instead he'd brought tears to her eyes again. "I'm sorry. No one likes being seen in their gardening clothes. These are my composing clothes!" He ventured a smile, but her face remained tight, closed.

At last she managed to respond, "Maybe your occupation's cleaner than mine."

What was the matter with the woman? She let her hair get like that and now she was worried about her clothes? It didn't make sense. But then he remembered that she'd saved Tim's life and he bit back the thought.

"Look," he said, as patiently as he could, "we've got to eat. There's probably something in my freezer. Let's go and look, shall we?"

CHAPTER
FOURTEEN

Outside the front door of A&E, Owen stopped dead.

"Look," Rebecca said, biting her lip, "I'm being really selfish, aren't I? Of course we should eat round here. Then you can pop back to see he's all right before he settles down for the night. That's what you want, isn't it?"

"I suppose you're right," he said. "That wasn't why I stopped, though. It's because I've no idea where I left my car." He didn't look amused, he looked panic-stricken.

Apart from a big spread of parking spaces, there were other, smaller bays. And in the late dusk, all the cars looked the same.

"We'll just have to walk systematically along the rows," she said. "What sort is it?"

"A Volvo. A Volvo estate."

"Well, that shouldn't be all that difficult, then."

"Don't you believe it. There are a lot of dowagers in Devon! Now, will you go this way and I'll got that?" He told her the number. "And whichever finds it comes back here and yells!"

She nodded. "Fine." But it wasn't fine at all. Her jacket, such as it was, was still hanging over the fork handle in her back garden. Her jumper wasn't just old and ugly, it was thin, no protection against the vicious wind. And her gardening shoes, the most dreadful of all her footwear, wouldn't stay on her feet if she tried to jog to keep warm.

Owen had been right. A lot of Volvos.

He was such an immaculate man. Why hadn't she at least been going into school when she'd found Tim? Then she'd have been clean and neat. But never stylish. Not like Owen. Composing clothes they might be, but those jeans didn't come for a fiver from Oxfam. And his sweater had a suggestion of class about it.

She'd walked past a Volvo without checking it. Back a few paces. Yes. This was the one. Without thinking, she put her fingers to her mouth and whistled.

Owen was still chuckling when he reached her. That was a skill Tim would die for. Where on earth had a woman like this learned it? One look at her told him to save any teasing till they were in the car and the heater was working.

"It wasn't just your bag I forgot, was it? I'm so sorry."

"You had other things on your mind," she said briefly.

Perhaps he should postpone the teasing indefinitely. He checked with the dash-board clock. Yes, there was plenty of time to get to the Exeter shops. Plenty. Well, enough. Dingles. There'd be something he could get her there. It was the least he could do, the very least.

"Here," he said, stretching over to the back seat. "All the best dowagers have car-rugs."

"In Birmingham," she said, "even dowagers don't leave stealable items on their back seats. Thanks." She swathed herself in it.

At least they were going against the flow of traffic. But then, even as he eased through the streets, he didn't think he could do it. How could he, a perfect stranger, say, look, I'll buy you a coat? It wasn't on, was it?

As he pulled into the multi-storey, he said, trying to sound like Tim, "Look, Rebecca. My son and I have really messed you around today. I didn't bring your bag, I didn't bring your coat. It's bloody freezing. Can I — what can I — ?"

"It's not a problem," she said, too quickly.

"You know it is. Tim — Tim would kill me if I let you die of pneumonia."

She said nothing. Maybe she was thinking as hard as he. He reflected. The house, the hair, the dreadful clothes. OK, gardening clothes. But he'd seen nothing when he was slamming her windows to suggest anything else was much better. And she was working at that school.

Was she poor?

The adjective surprised him. He'd have expected phrases such as "cash-flow crisis" or "strapped for cash" to come to mind. Like friends with school fees to pay. Needing a new car. That sort of thing. Nothing that couldn't be remedied.

What the hell could he do? Even she wouldn't balk at his paying for a meal. Perhaps he could compromise. A pub snack now — the return to see Tim as the excuse

118

— and then a meal at his house. Or would that imply he was embarrassed by her appearance? God, God, God!

She'd turned to face him and was studying his face. He looked up and smiled at her. "Sorry. I was miles away."

"Of course you were. Now, what about food?" She looked at her watch and pulled a face. "Not a very fashionable hour! Never mind, the lady looks a tramp!" She sang the last words. "And I really am too hungry for dinner at eight," she added, in case he'd missed the reference. With bravado rather than joy, he thought.

"I've really cocked it up," he said.

"You're entitled to. What about some pub grub? And then get back to Tim. And then home."

There was no mistaking it. The flatness of her voice. So what was causing it?

"Provided you let me stand you a really slap-up meal when we're both dressed for it! Deal?"

"Deal," she said, shaking his out stretched hand. But there was no enthusiasm there. But he could see her making an effort. "At least I," she said, getting out of the car, "am better off than you are!" She folded the rug diagonally and swirled it around her. Effort? The woman had style!

If ever a man was working hard, it was poor Owen. But what could she do? She didn't want to be drawn out, not about herself, not about her work, not about her cottage. If only her social skills were better, if only she knew how to parry and turn questions. At last she took the conversation by the scruff of its neck.

"Look, I'm sure that even being the librarian at Eton isn't really exciting. On the other hand, being a Hollywood composer might just be. What are you working on now?"

"Sumptuous film music," he said.

"The Korngold of Newton in Teign?"

He might have flickered an eyelid, just briefly: not the sort of thing a poor, plain widow might have said. And perhaps not all that many people would know about Korngold. But he said seriously, "Not that sumptuous. But it's a blockbuster movie, lots of emotion, nice feel-good ending."

"How much freedom do you get?" Why had she said "freedom" when she might just as well have said "licence". No prizes for guessing that, Rebecca.

"Oh, quite a lot. What you need is a good "hook" — a melody to capture the audience. Now, I'm not writing lush wallpaper, not just reacting to pretty scenery. What I'm trying to do is mirror the narrative drive with my music . . ." There. He'd started now. And she could have listened to him all night. And looked at him. He might have a good Welsh name, but his looks weren't what she'd have expected in a Welshman. No, those long elegant bones, the thick gold hair, and those remarkable blue eyes — they all suggested that some long ago Norseman had found his way into the principality and into the life of a childbearing woman. Although his face was striking in repose, when it was

120

animated it was — she groped for a word. None came. None adequate. Oh, he was so beautiful.

But was she really entranced by a pretty face? Or by the long, elegant fingers gesturing to make a point?

"So what sort of training did you have?" She must ask the right questions — couldn't bear to appear stupid.

"Oh, classical. Royal Academy and all that. I started off as a pianist but it didn't work out."

"No?" she prompted.

"I've got this lousy memory, see?" He grimaced. "And have you any idea how many notes there are to remember in — say — a Rachmaninov concerto?"

"A lot. And you have to put them all in the right order and play them at the right speed and loudly and quietly enough!"

"And do it all before a critical audience. God knows why people feel cheated if the soloist needs a score. But they do." He stopped as if he'd been turned off. "I've been rabbiting on. I hope your chicken was better than this steak."

"Fine."

He raised a quizzical eyebrow. Perhaps it was him Tim had been trying to imitate, not Tony.

"OK, it wasn't as good as the Gayes'." She risked a grin, looking at him under her eyebrows.

"You've eaten with the Gayes?"

Why did he sound so astonished? "They've been very kind to me. Both of them." Damn. That implied she'd needed kindness.

"They're very good people," he said, nodding the point home and smiling. "Look, do you fancy a sweet, or should we pop back to the hospital?"

She would have killed for a sweet if there'd been the remotest possibility of one tasting as good as the illustration in the menu looked. But he was already fishing out a credit card.

"Let's go and see Tim," she said.

He was sure her insistence that she needed a loo was only an excuse to give him a few minutes alone with Tim. And he was grateful for it.

Tim was drowsing, but opened his eyes as Owen took his hand. "I thought you were going home."

"We — I wanted to make sure they were treating you OK."

"Better than Low Ash! Well, the beds are. But it's a bit too dramatic. Guy over there had a cardiac arrest." Tim pointed.

"You're joking!"

"No. Don't think so. Though I am a bit woozy. Hey, you will look after her, won't you? We don't think she eats enough. You should see her kitchen. And she — oh, look!"

Owen turned. There was Rebecca, still wearing the car-rug, but with one end flung casually over the opposite shoulder.

She smiled, and walked forward as if unsure of her welcome.

"Becky — Mrs W — you look really good!"

Tim was right. The cold air — or was it the food and wine — had brought colour to her cheeks. And the dark blue of the travel rug emphasised the colour of her eyes. Owen started to his feet.

At least Tim had the presence of mind to do the right thing: he held out his hands to her. "Why haven't you worn that before?"

"Because it's your father's car-rug."

"Well, it's great. You should get a proper coat that colour. And get rid of all those nasty light-brown things. Go and get some nice blue shirts."

Her face had hardly changed but Tim must have registered something. "Oh, Becky, I mean Mrs W — I'm so sorry. I didn't mean — I know you can't. Not with what Payne-in-the-Arse pays you. Tony found out . . . Oh, Dad" — by now he was near to tears — "at least she can keep the rug, can't she?"

"It's OK, love, it's OK. And forget the Mrs W bit, eh? It's nicer being Becky." She had leaned forward and pulled him close. "Don't worry about it. Nothing to worry about." She let him sink gradually back on to the pillow. "There. You try and sleep now. And you'll be able to go back home tomorrow. Just close your eyes." She stroked back his hair. "There. Night, night, love." It was only when his eyes were drooping that she touched a kiss to his forehead, before turning and walking quickly from the ward.

Owen let her go. He might have his son to himself for a few minutes, but there was now someone else sharing Tim's affections. And he wasn't at all sure how he felt about it.

CHAPTER
FIFTEEN

If only her brain would work. If only it wouldn't knit itself up in complications.

Rebecca watched Owen cautiously. He seemed to be enjoying himself, relaxed and silent at the wheel, driving through the outskirts of Exeter. Once he looked at her and smiled briefly, as if content that he didn't have to say anything. She'd managed to smile back, knowing that in the dark he wouldn't have those clothes, that hair inflicted on him. She would have liked to stay like this. For ever.

But eventually their route would take them past her cottage. What if he wanted simply to drop her off there? How could she face the rest of the evening on her own? Flat? The word didn't approach what she'd feel. Or would he expect to come in? And how could she bear his inspection of the place? And of her? And if he didn't stop, if he took her straight up to his house, how would she survive there? Damn Rupert, and his fifteen years of control! Here she was, a woman of thirty-five, and she didn't know how to behave in a simple social situation, the sort of thing a kid of sixteen could cope with.

Except this was scarcely simple. And she was no longer sixteen.

He was slowing down for an island. "Which way? The coast road or the A road?"

Caught off guard, she said, "Oh, the coast road. You know, I haven't seen the sea since I arrived!"

He smiled. "The coast road it shall be, then." He turned left. "Not that you'll see much sea for a few miles yet. In fact, the road runs parallel to the Exe just along here, but you don't get to see much of it. In fact, you don't see much of anything at all, what with hills, high hedges, and masses of building."

"You'll think me really silly," she blurted. "But if there were somewhere you could stop. Quite close to the sea. Just for a minute." Damn, she sounded like a child pleading.

"Want a paddle?" He didn't sound sarcastic, just amused.

"Love one! But I've forgotten my wet suit," she batted back. But why not? Just because Rupert would have disapproved . . .

"Tim always likes this way best. Sometimes we stop in a little place called Dawlish. He's too grown up to admit it now, but he used to love feeding the ducks there. Always wanted to catch and cuddle a duckling. They moved just a bit too fast, though. Always. So I bought him a toy one. They were inseparable. Until he went to Low Ash, in fact. It sits on his pillow waiting for him to come home." His voice cracked.

"You'll have to tell it he'll be back tomorrow night," she said, holding back tears too.

125

He dropped a hand from the steering wheel on to hers, clasped in her lap. "I —" he removed the hand, checked his mirror and pulled over to a lay-by. "Rebecca: I — I — this should be so easy — I just want to say how grateful I am for what you've done today. All of it. Start to finish. You saved Tim's life and you've kept me going. I shall never be able to begin to thank you."

"I just happened to be there —" she began lightly.

"You happened to be there because even though he was knocked half-silly he knew he wanted to be with you." He took her hand again and raised it to his lips. "Thank you." Still holding it, he said, "I can never repay this debt. Ever. But if ever there's anything I can do — big, small, whatever — you will, won't you, please, just . . . just tell me."

The words came out of her mouth. "Tim's the son I never had." But then they stopped. What she'd meant to say was that there was no debt, no obligation.

Perhaps Owen understood. He kissed her hand again, replaced it in her lap, and started the car.

"There," Owen said, applying the handbrake as he pulled up in a street with shops one side, some sort of park the other. "Dawlish. Complete with black swans, fairy-lights over the brook — that's what they call that stream — and ducks. It's quite sheltered here. We could have a really close look at the sea, if you don't mind walking. Only a hundred yards."

"Try stopping me. Just to see it. Only for a minute, though. Unless you've got another rug? For yourself. Surely the best-equipped dowagers have two?"

126

He slapped his forehead and opened the boot. "My driftwood-collecting Barbour," he said. "God knows how old it is." He shrugged it on. All that emotion had left a dreadful vacuum. How on earth was she managing — all of a sudden — to seem so normal, so prosaic? There she was, wearing that bloody rug as if it were high fashion, and peering round for the beach, excited as a child.

"Ducks first," he said firmly, pointing to a wooden shed on the other side of the road. "Look, there's a little hatchery there. That wooden shed. You see, the one with the light on. It's for orphans. It's very busy in the spring."

There was a late brood of ducklings, soft and vulnerable, huddling together under a lamp.

"But you still can't touch them," she said, her hand flat against the glass.

The gesture, the tone of her voice, tore at his heart. What had happened to this woman?

Funny, the way the mouth worked on its own, sometimes. Mind you, it said more sensible things than the brain wanted it to say. Not the brain. The body. All Rebecca's body wanted to say was, "take me to bed with you now." She'd never chosen celibacy. More had it thrust upon her. Except thrust was completely the wrong verb! She choked back laughter.

He turned to her. No, she could hardly explain, could she. Though she wanted to tell him all about it, all about those fifteen years. All. So he'd understand. Everything.

But not now. She set off along the stone breakwater. It led straight to a moon-track across the sea. If she walked without hesitation she could follow the path all the way to the moon.

But not in these shoes. The dips and hollows in the great granite blocks were full of sea water — there was even weed in some of them. Well, the shoes might have helped her start on the garden, might have stamped out the bonfire — but now they were awash.

She kicked them off and hurled them as far as she could into the sea.

"That's the trouble with grand gestures," she said five minutes later, picking her way with comically exaggerated caution across the coarse sand.

Owen laughed. "Tell you what," he said, "I could always carry you back." She wouldn't weigh much, would she? And it would have stopped her poor white feet getting hurt.

"And how would your grand gesture end? A week flat on your back with a slipped disc? But you could bring the car a bit nearer."

No wonder Tim liked her. "OK. Provided you'll indulge me later on."

"Indulge you?" Her voice was sharp, then she seemed to control it again. "You want to throw your shoes in the sea? Be my guest. But don't say I didn't warn you."

"OK. I'll take your advice. Provided we can pick up fish and chips on the way home. There's this place Tim and I always go to . . ." Yes, he supposed it was one way to keep your mind off sex, to talk about food.

All these years — OK, not celibate, but near enough — and he wanted this woman, now. This plain, scruffy woman. Why not reach out for her? Kiss her?

He'd never had any doubts in the past. Not many. And none that the women in question hadn't been quick to resolve. And then partings had always been civilised. No hard feelings. He was still good friends with most of his lovers. But Rebecca . . . She wouldn't be able to kiss him goodbye and hop off to the South of France to cheer herself up with a shopping spree. No, she was as vulnerable as a virgin. If he were to bed her, he'd better be sure he wanted the relationship to last. Or Tim would never forgive him.

So what would happen now? She felt utterly powerless. Whatever they did would have to be Owen's decision. She would simply acquiesce. Go with the flow, that was the term. She clasped the bag of fish and chips. Yes, they'd have to eat it somewhere, and she'd have to sleep somewhere, and she'd have to get up and go into work. But none of this was in her hands now.

"There's a car opposite your cottage," Owen said. "Looks like Clifford-Payne's Saab." He pulled in behind it. "Just the chance I wanted." He was already out of the car when he turned to her. "You're sure you want to come too?"

"What do you bloody take me for?"

"You've got no shoes on."

"No more I have. And my tights are in shreds. That doesn't mean I don't want to speak to him." She set off across the road. Raising her voice, she called him. "Clifford!"

CHAPTER
SIXTEEN

"Mrs Wildbore! Wherever have you been? And in that state. Good God, woman, where are your shoes?" Clifford shone his torch full on her, its powerful beam sweeping her from head to foot. It returned to her face, dazzling her.

"Lower the torch, Clifford. I can't see to open the door." Rebecca fumbled through her pockets. Where on earth were her keys? Ah! Of course!

"Allow me," Owen said, his voice like ice. He leant between them, opened the door with a hard shove of the shoulder, and stood back to let her through, passing her the keys as she went.

The room was bitterly cold, of course, and smelt of vomit as well as damp.

Clifford stepped in, but changed his mind about closing the door. "Mrs Wildbore, I would like an explanation of this afternoon's events," he began.

"On the contrary," Owen said, "I — Mrs Wildbore and I — would like an explanation of this afternoon's events."

Whatever happened between them, she would always treasure that small but vital correction.

"There is no explanation to give. Not on my part. Your son was seen leaving the rugby field and heading for this cottage. He has not been seen since."

"Nor would he have been," Owen said, before she could reply. And while the last thing she wanted was for him to fight her battles, perhaps it was his right to fight this particular one. "Unless you'd happened to call at the Royal Devon and Exeter Hospital, that is. You'll find him in the A&E ward, if you care to go looking."

Clifford went pale. Though the word he would have chosen would surely have been "blenched". And then he flushed. "And what is your part in this nonsense, Mrs Wildbore?"

Again Owen stepped in. "Mrs Wildbore saved my son's life. And, incidentally, the reputation of your school, Clifford-Payne. You owe her a debt of gratitude almost as great as the one I owe her."

Clifford flushed more deeply. "What are you implying?"

"I'm not implying anything. I'm saying that whoever was supervising games wasn't doing a very thorough job. Any more than your matron did last year. The one who gave syrup of figs to the boy with peritonitis," he added, aside to her. "Poor kid." He made a sharp gesture: the boy must have died.

"I've no idea what you're talking about," Clifford said.

"Go back to school and talk to the games master. You'll find out soon enough. As will my solicitor."

"It's Mrs Wildbore I wish to speak to." Payne's eyes raked her, taking in the hair, the rug, the shredded

131

tights. "As a member of my staff, Mrs Wildbore, you are answerable to me. And I am waiting to hear why you made no effort to contact the school. We are, as even you must be aware, *in loco parentis*."

No, she wouldn't flinch. She said quietly, "On the contrary, I did try to phone the school. As soon as I'd called an ambulance and phoned Mr Griffiths. I hung on and on, but there was no reply. And Tim became too ill to leave at all."

By rights, he should have deflated. But he said nastily, "Easy to say, impossible, I'm afraid, to prove. I'll bid you goodnight, Mr Griffiths. Mrs Wildbore, I shall leave you to determine where your loyalties would sensibly lie."

He left, thwarted only by the door in his effort to make a dignified exit.

In the silence that followed, Rebecca would always swear the only sound was yet another ladder zapping up her leg.

Then Owen raised his right hand flat towards her. She'd seen Afro-Caribbean students doing that at home. She raised hers to match. And laughed with him as they swooped them together.

Then there was another silence. He looked around him, pulling a face and huddling closer into his Barbour. "No central heating?"

"No central heating. No nothing, really. Except I do have hot water, thanks to George Gaye. And a load of paint ready to apply to the walls. And George has promised me an off-cut of the staff room carpet, provided I promise to deny Clifford access to my

132

bedroom." Eyes dancing, she rolled the words generously about her mouth. "I said I thought I could manage that."

He grunted.

She made a decision. "What you have to understand, Owen, is that I have nothing. Absolutely nothing. I'm utterly dependent on Clifford. This — this hovel — is the only place I have to live. These dreadful clothes are all I have. My hair is like this" — she grabbed an offending handful — "because I can't afford to have it cut. It used to be my one luxury, a regular haircut. It's too fine to put up, too thick to tie back. Even Rupert admitted that. Now, excuse me — I need some new tights." She ran past him, up the stairs, ashamed to let him see her tears. She hoped they tears of were anger, not self-pity.

Her hands were shaking so much she could scarcely peel her clothes off. Somewhere she had some opaque black tights. Stylish and warm. Excellent. And there was a skirt that looked nice with them. And a jumper. There. That was better.

She could hear him running water in the kitchen. What on earth could he be doing? And then she heard the faint sound of scrubbing — he was cleaning her carpet! If he'd been high in her estimation before, he soared now. Rupert had never lifted a finger in the house.

Which shoes? Well, hardly any contest. Black tights, black shoes. She rubbed them quickly with the discarded skirt, slipped them on and ran downstairs.

★ ★ ★

"I don't hold out many hopes," Owen said cheerfully, popping a plate of chips in his microwave. "They'll be like a cup of tea. Warm and wet."

"Better than cold and wet," she said. "And much as I'd have liked to feed them to the ducks —"

"You can't feed the ducks on *chips*!" he declared, his voice dripping mock outrage. "Wholemeal bread. That's what Dawlish ducks get."

"You're joking!"

"Would I joke about something like that? Let's see if these are OK now. Hmm, not bad. What do you think? Kitchen table or living-room? With some music?"

"Elbows on kitchen table for chips." Some kitchen, some table. And it was so warm in here. Such luxury.

"Music later?" he asked.

"Try keeping me from it!"

He grinned, dividing the chips and heating the fish. "Vinegar in that cupboard there. Lemon juice if you prefer it in the fridge. Salt and pepper on the table." He passed cutlery. "Funny how stress makes you so hungry!"

"I'm always hungry!"

Something had happened to her during that encounter with Clifford-Payne, hadn't it? Something had clicked inside. He'd no idea what. But suddenly she was easier with him, more relaxed than he'd dared to hope. And he with her. Perhaps it was the wine. He sloshed more in both glasses. Not that he wanted to get her drunk. And there was no way he'd risk his licence.

It was only when they were eating he asked what he'd wanted to ask at the cottage. "Tell me, Rebecca. How did things get — like this?"

She took a mouthful of wine and savoured it. It was better than anything Rupert had ever bought, even for one of Clifford's visits. "Because I was very young and naive. I came from a village much smaller than this. I was a first generation university student, although it was the norm by then for the outside world. And this lecturer made a fuss of me. Not sexually. Better if he had. But he talked up my ability. Got me transferred from joint honours to single honours. Gradually weaned me from the friends I'd made. Got me helping with his research in the name of helping me with mine. Made sure I got a First, then talked me out of doing a Ph.D. Married me. Rather like Casaubon in *Middlemarch* marrying Dorothea. And he set about eroding my confidence. I don't even know if it was deliberate. Confidence about cooking. Clothes. Driving. All the normal things. And then — and I really think he was obsessed with his work, I don't think it was deliberate cruelty — he cut and cut away at my allowance. All his money was going on the bloody Coote Society. Oh, Coote — an early dictionary-compiler, very much earlier than Johnson."

He shook his head. He was so appalled he didn't think he dared speak.

"Of course you've never heard of him. No one's ever heard of him. In 1596 he brought out *The Englishe Scholemaster, teaching all his scholars of what age soever* . . . You don't really want me to go on, do you?"

"I'm sure you could." He topped up her wine. "I have to ask: why did you put up with it?"

135

"By the time he'd finished with me I didn't realise I had an option. Plus he and Clifford were bosom-buddies. Whenever Clifford came to stay, he reinforced Rupert's message. That I was generally dim, stupid and ugly, but I had my uses as a researcher. And as unpaid secretary of the Coote Society."

"The bastard." He found he was clenching his fists.

She nodded. "That's right. The bastard. There's more. But —"

He leaned across and covered her hands, clasped tightly on the table. "If you want to tell it, I want to hear it. But why not come into the living-room? It's much more comfortable."

"This is more a hard table than a comfy sofa narrative. This summer just gone, Rupert died."

"Old age?"

"No. A number 63 bus. He never looked where he was going. He'd made a will. In the will . . ." She swallowed hard. "In the will, he left everything to the Coote Society or to the university. The Wildbore Prize. To keep his memory green."

"But surely the Law —"

"The Law says he can do what he wants. I can appeal, of course. But to go to law in these enlightened times you need money."

"What about legal aid?"

"I'm not paid much per hour, but I work a lot of hours. And apparently the fact the job comes with accommodation has to be taken into account. So I'm not eligible for legal aid I gather, though I may have been misinformed —"

"Payne told you!"

"How did you guess? It's something I shall check up on. Or I shall try to find a solicitor to take me on on a no-win, no-fee basis. Now I have the will — sorry about the pun — to do it."

"But why didn't you before? Rebecca." He stopped short. He could hardly remind her how thin, how scruffy she was. She knew that already, poor woman.

She shrugged. "I wasn't sure if I dared. After all, I'd been under Rupert's thumb all those years. And then, when I knew I did, I heard this silly whisper of pride telling me not to soil myself with anything of his. But I shall set about it as soon as I can. Now." She yawned, enormously, pushing the hair right off her face and rubbing her hands over her ears, right down her throat. They came to rest at the back of her neck. She eased her head back, slowly, as if it were too heavy to hold up any longer. He was sure she didn't mean it as a come-on, but he found it unbearably erotic. "All the food, all the drink," she said, with a smile that just missed being an apology.

Was it an invitation?

"On top of quite a day. Come on through." Automatically he picked up the glasses and the bottle. She didn't protest. How did she expect the evening to end? She must know he shouldn't drive, not with half a bottle of wine inside him. Did she want to sleep with him? How would she feel if he suggested it? How would she feel if he didn't?

Jesus, what was the matter with him! Had her lack of confidence infected him? It was just a matter of sitting

137

beside her and kissing her. And letting their bodies decide.

They were halfway across the hall when she stopped in her tracks.

"Tony!" she said.

"What about Tony?" He hoped he didn't sound as exasperated as he felt.

"He ought to know about Tim. Being all right. We didn't exactly fill Clifford with cheer, did we?"

He gave a bark of laughter. "Did you expect me to?"

"I'd rather Clifford went to bed expecting every moment to be Tim's last. But not Tony. Tony's his friend."

Well, however he'd expected the evening to go, he hadn't planned on this. Blast the ever-charming Tony. He always managed to get everyone to dance to his tune, didn't he?

"Do you want to phone — though I can't imagine they'd be happy him having a call at this time of night."

"I don't think lights out is till eleven thirty for the sixth-formers, is it? But the call should come from you, Owen. Not me." She looked at him steadily, as if daring him to make her spell it out.

He managed a rueful grin.

He was just looking up the number when there was a tremendous knocking at the front door.

For God's sake! Something wrong with Tim? The police come to break the news? He was across the hall in a second, flinging open the door.

To Tony.

So now the three of them were sitting in the kitchen, glasses in hand. But Tony, despite the cheese sandwich he'd cadged, was already looking at his watch.

And now he was on his feet. "So you will let me know when I can come up, won't you, Owen? I mean — he's a nice kid."

Owen said, sounding ungracious even to his own ears, "Well, he'll have to be quiet for some days. But of course I'll keep you informed." He forced cordiality into his voice. After all, the lad was breaking all sorts of rules to be here. God knew what his father would say. "You'll be able to phone him tomorrow, anyway. And come up over the weekend, some time. Maybe for lunch. How about Sunday?" He led the way into the hall, Rebecca following.

"That'd be great!" There was no mistaking the way the boy's eyes lit up. "You've no idea how crap veggie Sunday lunch can be!"

"I give you fair warning — it'll probably be pretty crap here. I can sizzle a steak with the best of them, but —"

"Did you say steak, mate? I'll turn carnivore for the day. Now, Rebecca, do you want me to walk down with you?" He spoke easily, familiarly. As if he were as close to her as Tim was. Closer than himself. "I know this is the countryside and everything but it's still dodgy on your own."

Shit, it was the obvious answer. Obvious. Except it was the last one he wanted. And she was going to say yes, wasn't she, because she knew exactly how much he'd had to drink. Whichever bed Rebecca ended up in, his or the spare room one, he didn't want it to be that vile damp one.

And he didn't want her escort to it to be Tony. Hell, the boy could charm his way the wrong way round a revolving door, couldn't he?

"I'll run you both down," he said curtly, reaching her jacket from the newel post. "And you'd be warmer in the blanket than in that, you know." He shook it out for her, and then flicked it diagonally in half, so she could wear it as she had before. She turned so he could put it across her shoulders, and then faced him again.

She put her hand on his arm. He stared at it, then, in response to its light pressure, looked up.

"Stay by the phone. Just in case." Her eyes filled. They were as blue as Tim's, but a shade lighter. How did those eyes come with that hair? "But you would, wouldn't you — phone me? Whatever time?"

"Of course. You'll come and eat with us tomorrow? Tim and me?" He bit his lip: he didn't mean to snub Tony, but there was no doubt the boy would notice the difference in their invitations.

"Try and stop me. But — I know you'll be phoning the hospital in the morning — you will let me know how he's going on?"

"Try and stop me!" What he wanted to do was take her in his arms. What he'd better do was send them both on their way. "OK. Mind how you go, both of you. We don't want that stalker getting anywhere near you."

"See you, Owen. And all the best to Tim." Tony suddenly reached for Owen's hand, shaking it one man to another. Yes, there were tears in his eyes, weren't

140

there? Time for a man-to-man hug, then. At last they pushed apart.

Easy, then. A repeat performance with Rebecca. Plus a kiss. On the cheek? She was so thin and bony in his arms. But taller than he'd realised. And there was no doubt she was hugging him back. He grew hard against her. Her eyes widened, but he couldn't read them.

She reached up and held his face a moment. "You take care, now. See you tomorrow." And she kissed him not on the cheek, but on the lips.

CHAPTER
SEVENTEEN

They walked down the moonlit drive in silence. Tony's face was stern: he was probably reflecting on Tim's injury and his father's reaction to it. Rebecca was wondering whether she was grateful or otherwise for Tony's interruption and offer. My God, how she'd wanted to kiss Owen, to hold him. Even now, in the cold night air, the thought of him made her legs weak. Which brought her back sharply to the present: the asphalt was broken and pot-holed in places. Both of them had better watch where they were putting their feet.

The lane which the drive led into wasn't much wider. At least they'd get plenty of warning of approaching cars — the sound would travel in the almost still air. From time to time one of them would crunch a twig or kick a stone. A fox padded across their path. In the woods behind Owen's house an owl — two sorts of owl — hooted.

At last they could see the streetlights of the village. Off to the right a footpath cut through to the school.

"Off you go, Tony," she said. "I'll be fine from here. It's only a step. And you're going to be in all sorts of trouble."

"Might as well be in one more, then, hadn't I? No, Rebecca, this peeping Tom character — you've got to take him seriously. You know what the psychologists say. Sex offenders start with comparatively trivial things. And they build up. Wouldn't want anything to — to happen to you," he finished, awkwardly.

"No. One day's drama's enough." She paused. All the talk at Owen's had been about Tim and his chances of recovery. "What did they say at the school about Tim?"

"Said he'd skived, didn't they? But I'd seen him change for rugger. And the rugger coach might have been a great player — twenty years ago, that is! — but he's a crap teacher. Vicious bugger, too. And I reckon he was looking shifty. So I cornered one of the kids. Nothing heavy, like. Just enough to find a few details. Enough to talk to C — well, his name is Hunt, so you can guess what we call him."

"Indeed," she said, dryly. "And then?"

"I guess I panicked. You see, I didn't know which way he'd gone. But then George Gaye said there'd been an ambulance outside your house, and Owen's car. And that Owen had driven off on his own — like the clappers. And I knew you weren't in. So I put two and two together. Phoned the hospital. Bingo. So though the Old Bastard was glad he could call off a search, he wasn't a happy bunny at all."

"So he did know about Tim being in hospital?"

"I told you. About — what, three this afternoon?"

"And about my part in it?"

"Well — I didn't want to push that bit too much. I knew he wouldn't like it. He — it doesn't do to get on the wrong side of him, Becky. Believe me."

She looked sharply at him. She knew things between them must be bad — imagine having to call your own father "sir"! — but this sounded far worse than mutual antipathy. Why on earth couldn't he go and live with his mother? Someone who might love him? But what had Clifford told her about his ex-wife? That she was a hard-drinking nymphomaniac? Well, she rather doubted that. Now she'd seen how Clifford stretched the truth. "Oh, Tony —"

"It's OK," he said. "I can deal with him. I'm glad you were there for Tim," he added, as if keen to change the subject. "Must have been . . . tricky."

"Oh, it was OK, once the ambulance had arrived, that is. How soon did you know it wasn't serious?"

"Only when I saw you two tonight. A&E wouldn't give any details at all, of course, since we're not related. Nor to the OB, I gather. And then you weren't back to ask. I thought that looked pretty bad. And I don't know what you said to the OB, but you didn't half put the wind up him. I'm glad to say."

By now her cottage loomed in the middle-distance. If only she could take him in, comfort him like a beaten dog.

"He's OK, Owen, isn't he?" he said. "Prefers my room to my company, but that's fair enough. And he doesn't half owe you: he thinks the sun shines out of Tim's arse."

"He seems nice enough." Should she have kissed him like that? Should she? Her lips throbbed briefly as if they remembered and wanted to do it again. Of course she should have done. And for much longer. Oh, God! Yes, and he'd wanted her!

"You should see his equipment!" Tony said reverently.

A schoolgirl voice yelled in her head that she'd already felt some of it. What if she started to giggle? It was so long since she'd touched alcohol she might well. She bit on the back of her index finger.

"State-of-the-art computer, recording equipment, keyboards," Tony continued. "The lot. God knows why. I mean. He's got bloody studios at his disposal, hasn't he? But some of his mates come to stay sometimes. You should see the cars. And the women. Christ!"

Women! Had someone punched her in the stomach? But of course he must have had — had relationships. Trying to control her voice, she asked, "Is he a widower? Divorced?"

"Divorced. I reckon he'd like to shack up with someone again to give Tim a bit of stability."

"Tim strikes me as very stable." She hoped her voice was.

"Sure. But he'd probably like a mum." Tony's voice tightened.

Poor kid. Poor, poor kid.

Now he was laughing, in a laddish sort of way. "You should see some of the totty Owen's brought home for his inspection. Not just tarts, top-class women. Film stars. I mean film and I mean stars. But Tim says his heart's never been in it. He's probably got someone tucked away in the States he doesn't want Tim to know about. I mean, a man like that — got an Oscar nomination for his last score, didn't he? — can pull any bird he fancies."

She could think of nothing to say. And her throat was so tight she was sure nothing more than a croak would emerge anyway. She took a deep breath. Thank goodness, they were at her gate.

She licked her lips. "Thanks, Tony. Now, push off fast." She opened her gate and walked through.

"Yeah. Better had."

"Tim will be all right. I promise."

He stayed where he was, shoulders hunched, face averted. Absent mother, worse father. On impulse she stepped into the lane again and hugged him. It was a second before he returned the hug. And then he broke away and set off as fast as he could up the hill. He didn't look back.

Nor did she expect him to.

Oh, yes. There was plenty she could blame for not being able to sleep. The drama of the day: the food; the wine; the brisk walk; the icy coldness of the house; the fact that the only warm bit of bed was the part she was in. Any one of those might have kept her awake.

But even in the most comfortable circumstances she would have lain hot-eyed and sleepless. Except perhaps in Owen's bed.

You heard what Tony said, she told herself. *The man's out of your league. No, out of your universe. His talent. His looks. His friends. His other women. Talk about* King Cophetua and the Beggar Maid.

Except she was no maid. She was no longer even young. She was plain. She was unemployable. Her clothes smelt of damp. She probably smelt of damp.

He'd seemed to want her company. *Of course the poor man did. He needed anyone's company after what he'd been through. He's probably taken Tim's duckling to bed.*

And he'd seemed truly grateful to her. *Fine. Of course he was grateful. Do you really want someone to seek you out simply because he's grateful? No, a nice bunch of flowers tomorrow, and that's it, Becky.*

What about his erection when they'd kissed? *Of course he'd have wanted sex. It's a normal human reaction to the end of a terrifying situation. That's probably why you want sex.*

Oh, yes, she'd wanted sex. It was astonishing that a body that had been dormant for so long could wake up so very quickly.

No, it isn't. Never heard of Merry Widows? What do you think they want? But at least they don't want sex with teenage boys!

She hadn't — she didn't . . . *Well, why did you grab him, then?*

All she'd wanted to do was comfort him — he'd had a bad day too. Just to hug him.

Hug? Some hug for the poor lad to end with an erection as hard as Owen's!

CHAPTER
EIGHTEEN

Eight fifteen. The phone? The phone! Rebecca was out of bed and down the stairs. It had to be about Tim, didn't it? It had to be Owen!

His voice was rather deeper on the phone than she'd expected. "Rebecca? He's fine. He's had a good night. He's fine."

"I'm so glad." If she wasn't careful she'd cry with relief.

"Are you all right? I didn't wake you, did I?" His voice sounded anxious.

She rallied. "It's a good job you did! Look at the time!"

"You're going in to work today? After the way Payne spoke to you last night?"

"I can't afford to be a prima donna," she said flatly.

"What time can you come up this evening? We never settled a time, did we?"

She had to be sensible. "Look, are you sure — I mean, I don't suppose you —"

"I'll collect you at six," he overrode her. "If that's not too early. It's just I thought Tim might not feel as bright as he says he feels — and he'll need lots of rest."

"Don't even think about leaving him on his own. I never told you — I've got a bike!" So he could drink, if he wanted, without having to worry about getting her home.

"It's a bit of a hill," he said doubtfully.

"It's a lot of a hill, and I may need a bottle of embrocation tomorrow!"

His laugh was like music. "I'll treat you to a bottle of the vet's finest!"

If she'd raised Tim from the dead, she couldn't have been treated with greater awe and respect. The boys gave way in silence as she walked through the corridors. Swine might have sneered, but there was a tight little bunch of late chrysanths in a jam jar on her desk. *Congratulations, my dear Rebecca — and thanks. Reg Sowerby*. Nothing — nothing at all — from Clifford. Not even a note sacking her. Soon Cavendish appeared.

"Look, Mrs Wildbore — Rebecca! — it sounds as if you did wonders yesterday. And we're all — well, proud to have you on the staff."

She flushed. "Thanks."

"Now, one or two of us thought we should have a little celebration. What about this evening?"

"I'm booked, I'm afraid." Had she ever been able to say that, ever, ever, before?

"Tomorrow — no, we've got an away game on Saturday — got to set a good example. How about Monday?"

This was no big deal. Just a drink with some of the men she knew by sight and name, now, but who had never done more than exchange the fewest of words. It would be stand-offish to turn down the invitation. And it wasn't as if she had anything else to look forward to, was it?

"Monday would be fine," she said. "What time do we all meet up and where?"

"Er — now, don't get me wrong, but I've an idea the Chief isn't going to be too keen on the idea. So we're keeping this quiet." He tapped the side of his nose. "I'll collect you from your cottage. We'll go on from there."

Were they men or were they mice? Still, with an invitation in the offing, this was not the time to be critical. She smiled. "Fine. What time?"

"How about eightish? Ah, looks as if you've got a bit of a rush. See you later."

Well, she supposed five boys might just constitute a rush. Just.

As she closed up for lunch — at nearly twelve thirty, despite what Sowerby had said — Tony appeared. She'd wondered why he hadn't come earlier, asking for news of Tim. But perhaps he'd phoned Owen — after all, there was no reason why he shouldn't. He looked at her quizzically. "Everything OK, Becky?"

"Fine. Why?

"Just wondering why you were still here."

"Still here?"

"Well, you're on unpaid overtime for a start. But then everything's shut down for the day. God," he sighed, "the Chief Master hasn't forgotten to tell you, has he?" His voice dripped irony. "There's this

150

cross-country run this afternoon. The whole school's either watching or running."

"You're running?"

"Yeah. Will you be at the finishing line?"

"You bet." An embryo idea started to grow. "If I can, that is," she added. "Or — Tony, I may not be. It isn't early closing or anything this afternoon, is it?"

"Going to melt some plastic, are you? Good on you, Becky!"

But his voice was flat: perhaps he had wanted her there. She looked up quickly: what on earth could she say? But he was already strolling away, hands in pockets, whistling illicitly under his breath.

OK, so it was crazy to cycle all the way into Newton Abbot. And her muscles and joints would certainly pay for it. Heavily. But if there were the remotest chance that she could find someone to tackle her hair, it would be worth excruciating stiffness for a week. At least it was mostly down hill on the way — the vital thing was to allow time to find a salon. She zipped her credit card — she'd only ever used it to back cheques, before — into her pocket, and set off as unencumbered as she could.

How on earth do you choose a good hairdresser, except by word of mouth? She would avoid the really old-fashioned Doreens of this world, sitting on back-street corners, windows swathed in pink net. She would equally avoid those that looked as if you had to pay to walk in — all white tiles and spindly black furniture. But ultimately she would have to go to whoever would take her. She could risk an appointment as late as three thirty. Anything after that and she'd be late at Owen's.

The first three she tried were completely booked. But a fourth — more expensive than she'd wanted — would squeeze her in. At three. So she had time to kill, a credit card in her pocket and an attractive-looking department store across the way. For once, just this once, if Owen held her, he would not smell musty clothes. Even if it meant buying new bras and pants.

She must have been off her head. For two pins she'd skip the hair appointment — just bolt for home. How she'd ever pay off the card, she'd no idea. It wasn't as if she could sell anything. The only thing of any value was her cello, now in the hands of Margaret's daughter, who had probably come to think of it as her own. No, she mustn't think about that now. She had to think about her next move. Make herself go home.

But as she unchained the bike from one set of railings and looked for another set, she knew she was going to do it. Even if it meant depriving Rupert's niece, whose family could well afford to buy it or a better cello. Better, with their money. She plunged into the salon, accepted a cup of pallid tea, and submitted to the stylist's hands. It would all be worth it if only as soon as he saw her Owen's eyes lit up and he took her into his arms.

The front door opened at last. Tim flew at her, like a child, and then drew back. Another day nearer to manhood, even for Tim. He looked down at his pyjamas and slippers, and touched a finger to his lips.

"Dad'll kill me for coming out."

"Get back in then. Or I will, too."

"What, kill me?"

"Twice."

She was barely in the hall when Owen's voice came from the kitchen, "Get back on to the sofa, you little mongrel." He emerged, wiping his hands on a blue-and-white-striped apron. He looked drained: she wondered how much sleep he'd had.

"Hi, Rebecca," he said, almost absently kissing her cheek. "He's only allowed out on the proviso he keeps his feet up and stays quiet. And look at him."

Tim flapped a hand and retreated.

"And now the bloody garlic's burning!" Owen dashed for the kitchen.

So that was that. Nothing had registered, had it? Not the hair, the make-up, the new blue jacket. She took off the jacket and hung it on a spare peg. There was a convenient mirror, but she hardly bothered to look. All that effort. All that money. All that debt. All for a man who was simply grateful. Well, she should have known better.

Where now? Whom should she follow?

At least she should be sure of a welcome from Tim. Biting her lip she drifted into the living-room she'd never quite got to see the previous night.

Oh dear. It was one thing to fall in love with a rich man, another to fall in love with his home. She'd not realised from the exterior that the house was Georgian, but it had to be. The proportions, the fireplace, the furniture — this was a room you'd never want to leave. No wonder Owen put himself to all the inconvenience of travel if he had this to come home to.

She turned to Tim, now back on the sofa, under a duvet. She bit her lip again. Should she have returned the travelling rug? Tim had wanted her to keep it, but Tim wasn't Owen. Though he'd been the one to swathe her in it last night. He certainly wouldn't want it back in his house until she'd had it cleaned to eradicate every last trace of damp.

The duvet cover was blue, too. It brought out the blue of Tim's eyes — would he be as good looking as his father? Almost certainly. If in a slightly softer way. Meanwhile he was very pale, and looked sheepish as she perched beside him.

"You won't tell Dad, will you? He'll worry if he thinks I'm knocked up."

"Not a word shall pass my lips. Except you'd better stay put and get a bit of colour back if you want to convince him you're not. Why not close your eyes, have a bit of a zizz? You'll look better, then." For all she sounded cheerful and positive, she was worried sick. She'd heard patients could be slung out of hospital with more haste than judgement — what if he had a relapse?

She kissed his forehead and switched off the table lamp nearest him. "There. Snooze time."

And for her? Well, she'd better go and talk to Owen. And forget about falling in love with him. And forget that she'd bought the first new, non-charity shop outfit for ten years just for his benefit.

154

Owen grubbed inside the cupboard for the mop. Hell and hell and hell. The garlic had burned, so he'd had to start the whole thing again, he hadn't got the table laid yet, and there was no way he could ask Tim to do it, and he'd just knocked over the bottle of wine he'd had breathing. And he'd not even spoken to her yet. Or broken the news about the rest of this evening to her.

And now the bloody potatoes were boiling over.

"Shall I turn them off or turn them down?" It was Rebecca.

"Off, please. Altogether."

"Drain them?"

"Into that saucepan, please. There!" He rung out the mop and stowed it. It fell forward, smacking him sharply on the nose. "Shit!" He tested for damage — no, it was OK. What the hell must she think of him? It wasn't as if he didn't cook. It was a daily task when Tim was at home. And he'd cooked dinner for twelve without turning too many hairs. So what was happening to this simple supper for three? If he went and laid the table in the dining-room it would mean leaving her on her own. And the dining-room was a bit formal. Would she mind eating here? God, he was like a kid on his first date.

"Becky — I'm sorry about this. I meant to have it all ready." He turned to her at last. "Welcome." He was about to kiss her — cheek? lips? — when she backed away sharply.

"Where's your kitchen towel? And ice?"

She passed him a wodge of paper towel, and dug in the fridge.

"We're out of ice. Sorry. Anyway, it's stopping, I think. Hell, I got some blood on your top! Get it under the cold water tap now. I'll get you one of Tim's T-shirts."

He sprinted upstairs, using all the swear words he knew, and putting them in ever-new permutations. What the hell was wrong with him? And pray God he could find a clean T-shirt. Tim might have to be disciplined in such matters at school, but at home he simply dropped things on the floor, clean and dirty.

And would she be coy about him seeing her undressed? Should he knock, give her time to cover up?

He'd left the kitchen door wide open, of course. So he couldn't help seeing her back, as she stood at the sink, checking that the stain had gone. Couldn't help seeing the strong shoulders, the fine skin, and the little price tag left on her new bra.

"I can't tell you how sorry I am," he said, coming in, forgetting all about knocking. "Here. I hope it's clean. Look, if that's stained, you'll tell me, won't you?"

"It's fine. Is there somewhere I can leave it to drip dry?"

All so prosaic, so bloody prosaic. And the top was new, too: the remains of the plastic price loop must have been scratching like hell. He took a pair of scissors and snipped it off as she slipped the T-shirt over her head.

"Here. In the utility room. Otherwise known as the tip." He passed her a plastic hanger. "You do it. Or I shall drop it into a tin of paint the way my luck's running today. Oh, Becky. Let me say hello properly." A

156

tuft of her hair had been ruffled when she'd pulled off the top. He smoothed it down, and took her face between his hands. He was going to make quite sure she knew she was welcome — and more.

"Dad! Dad! Where are you? Phone, Dad. Ah, there you are. That geezer from the States for you."

"Shit!" He dotted the merest touch on her lips. "I'm coming! Get back on that sofa. Now."

So what should she do? Rebecca looked round the kitchen — a modern version of an old-fashioned farmhouse kitchen. The table was old, though. Real wood. And all the cupboard doors — she went round shutting the open ones gently — were wood, not chipboard. The recipe book Owen was working from was lodged in a piece of V-shaped perspex to prevent splash stains — rather too late. It was already marbled with grease. Chicken joints — with shallots and garlic and herbs, by the look and smell of them — sizzled in the tower oven. The potatoes still sat in their saucepan, the water they'd boiled in in another. He must be proposing to sauté or roast them, since they were only par-boiled. Much as she'd like to get stuck into the cooking — imagine using those lovely utensils! — she decided against it. It would mean burrowing for a pan, for oil and butter. What she could do was sort out some of the mess in the sink. The rubber gloves on the draining-board were too big, but she slipped them on anyway. What had her life come to, that she should enjoy washing up simply because hot water gushed from a tap? She dealt with the pile all too quickly. For good measure she wiped the working surfaces and the table. There.

There was no reason not to wash the salad. The end-of-season lettuce came complete with earth and slug trails: the smell reminded her of those she'd left behind in her garden in Birmingham. No. She mustn't think about the garden, in case she thought of other things, too.

And now what? Well, she could set the table. If she could lay her hands on cutlery? Well, there were enough knives and forks waiting to be dried. So she could do that. And then — why not — she sat at his table and immersed herself in his *Guardian*.

His face was like thunder when he came back in. She folded the paper quickly — was such a small thing too much of a liberty? But common sense, surfacing rather late in the day, told her his anger must have something to do with the phone call. In fact, as he took in the changes in the room his face was transformed, as if someone had switched on a lamp inside it.

"Oh, Becky," he said, "you are such a good woman. Why do you keep on making me grateful to you? First making Tim have a proper lie down. Now this. Here — you've only missed one thing." He produced glasses and flourished a bottle of champagne.

Grateful. Such a good, honest, decent word. Not the sort that went with champagne. "Grateful" went with cups of tea and kind handshakes. She wanted a word that went with his glowing eyes and slightly opened lips. Whatever she felt for him, she didn't expect to hear the word "love" yet. If ever. Desire? Lust? At least they were words with feeling.

But why should he feel those? For her? Tony could clearly understand Owen bedding any number of film stars, but had given not so much as a hint that Owen could fancy her. Except Owen had, hadn't he. For just one exciting moment.

No, he must have been thinking of the film stars.

Owen was peering at her, face troubled. "Or — or would you prefer sherry, or something."

She'd tried so hard, and he was offering her sherry! She made a huge effort. "Widow I may be, dowager I am not!"

For answer he put the bottle down and took her in his arms.

CHAPTER
NINETEEN

Tim wandered into the kitchen. He felt a lot better since that kip. Hungry, too. That could be the smell of the chicken. Dad's chicken was always good. It should impress Rebecca, too. Dad had better impress Rebecca. She'd certainly impressed Dad. All the way back from the hospital he'd been rabbiting on about her, probing for bits of information Tim might have forgotten to pass on. Her cottage, P.A., and even Tony. As if Tim hadn't already told him everything he knew last weekend.

Ah, well. It'd be worth it, if it would get them together. It had taken that bang on the head to make him see it, but he was now absolutely certain that if he had to have a stepmother, Rebecca was the one. And he did need a stepmother. He wouldn't be at home to keep an eye on his father for ever. Another three or four years and he'd be off to music school somewhere. He had an idea that Owen was seeing it that way himself. What he had to do now was make sure that Owen and Rebecca spent as much time as possible together. No problem.

So why was she wearing his Save the Dolphins T-shirt? God, what if it wasn't clean? Or if it had got tangled up with some of his socks?

"Hi," he said, "any idea when dinner will be ready?"

"Soon as I've cooked the spuds. And I suppose I can't persuade you to eat salad with the chicken?"

Hello. The old man had a hard-on. Better and better. And Becky was flushed.

"Frozen peas, please." He fished a packet from the freezer, pouring a liberal portion into the palm of his hand and eating them like peanuts.

"Nursery food," Owen said, passing a small saucepan. "Hang on, you're supposed to be lying down. At very least sitting."

"What happened to that nice top, Becky?" he asked, sitting down and eating a couple more peas.

"I bled all over it," Owen said, fussing with oil and butter.

"Not another of your nose-bleeds. When are you going to get the doctor to do something, Dad?" He turned to Rebecca. "He's so embarrassing. You're sitting in this restaurant and suddenly there's blood pouring down his face. Like something out of Dracula. You've forgotten to reach out the mustard."

Owen turned down the gas under the potatoes, plonked the mustard on the table, and sat down. "I've got some bad news. Oh, not life or death . . ." He smiled at them both. "But I've got to zap down to London. They want a score by next Wednesday. Just like that."

London! What about Rebecca? And wasn't someone supposed to be keeping an eye on him? He didn't fancy trusting Matron to do it. "Come off it, Dad. You've got proper contracts, these days. You don't have to do rush-jobs like that."

"I do with this one. It's the director I got the nomination with last time."

"For best film score," Tim explained. "Anyway, why's that bad news?" As if he didn't know.

"Because you, Tim, are going to have to go and stay with Grandma."

"Bloody hell! No!" But what about Rebecca?

"Bloody hell, yes. The medics only let you out provided you had round-the-clock supervision. So I'm terribly afraid —"

"I can look after myself!" Yes, he could.

"Any ordinary weekend you could. Or you'd be at school. But not after a bang like that."

"I'll go back to school then."

"And have Matron look after you?"

"Becky'll be there." Ah! That'd be his trump card.

"Becky'll be in the library."

"If it would help," Becky put in, looking from son to father, "I could sleep up here? And stay here over the weekend?"

"Yeah! Mrs Thingy could look after me tomorrow."

Owen was tempted. Tim could see he was. He was looking from him to Rebecca and back again.

"That would leave next week. It's too much to ask of you, Rebecca, and of Mrs Taylor. Especially Mrs Taylor. Tim could have blood-clots by the score and she'd never notice."

"It's certainly not too much to ask of me," Rebecca said, going red.

162

"You've done more than enough — I can't keep on letting you help me out. Oh, of course I could." He touched her hand. "I'd bloody pay to get you out of that cottage. And we've certainly enough spare rooms here. But Mrs Taylor is not you, Becky. And," he said in a voice meant to say that discussion was at an end, "I've already spoken to your Gran. We'll be off by six thirty tomorrow." He looked hard at Rebecca: Tim could have sworn he shook his head slightly. Behaving as if he was a kid and couldn't see!

"I don't want to go and that's final!" Tim yelled. Shit, he was afraid he was going to blub.

Rebecca got up and laid a hand on his forehead. "I'm afraid your dad's right. I'd much rather appoint myself chief slave, but I've got to go into work, and someone's got to keep an eye on you. How soon will you be back, Owen?"

Why was she gnawing at her lip? She was trying to sound all casual, but more like she was trying not to cry.

"Oh, by next weekend for sure. Guaranteed. All the invitations are out. Our bonfire party. That's another reason why I want Tim to be well. I'd hate him to miss that."

So would Tim. So would Rebecca, and she'd not been invited. He could tell from her face. "So long as Rebecca can come."

"Of course Rebecca can come. Now, everyone ready to eat?"

Owen looked at Rebecca. "I handled that very badly."

She made no attempt to deny it. She'd been at least as hurt and upset as Tim. And what was all this about a bonfire? Yes, she had an invitation, but it had been distinctly off-hand, as if he'd only asked her in order to shut Tim up. Was she OK to kiss, but not good enough to meet his friends?

"I've got worse to come, as well. I wanted . . . I wanted to get to know you this evening. I wanted . . . And now my sodding computer's thrown a wobbly and it won't talk to my e-mail so I've got to print stuff off sheet by sheet and fax it. And produce another ten minutes of music by eleven tonight. Fully orchestrated. And I cannot, cannot get out of it. I blow a whole contract if I do."

She set her coffee cup firmly in its saucer. "Show me how to work the printer and the fax."

"No, I can't ask you. Not another favour."

"I'm quite good at menial tasks, Owen. I might as well do them for you as for anyone else."

He looked straight at her, but she was picking at something on her trousers. Was she hurt? Or angry? Or both? Jesus Christ, what was the matter with him? She was so ashamed of her clothes she'd only been and bought new, hadn't she? New everything. He'd bet that in that event her panties were new. And all he'd done was bleed all over her new top. He'd never even praised her hairdo. Which wasn't at all bad, if not quite what he'd chosen for her.

How on earth was she going to pay for everything? Dare he offer to pay if she helped him tonight? The angle of her head told him that whatever he did would be wrong.

"Could you help me?" he asked, very humbly.

164

Her face still averted, she nodded.

He might call it a music room but in fact it was more like a lab or even a recording studio. One end, at least. There was a grand piano at the far end, plus a cello case, a filing cabinet marked SHEET MUSIC, and several music stands. But at this end were electronic amplifiers, loud-speakers, the sort of mixing equipment she'd seen on TV shots of recording studios, and a computer tower. The monitor was far bigger than Rupert's, and the printer looked more complicated than anything she'd used before. Beside that lot stood a fax machine.

Owen reached behind the fax machine. "Yes. They've done their bit. This is from the music editor," he said. "He's taken time measurements of each scene — each bit of scene action broken down to a third of a second. He's transferred the highlights to this sheet of manuscript paper — see, at the top? So I know whether to hit, relax, or reprise. Now I know the theme I'm using. All I've got to do is play with it so it fits that shape."

"All!"

"It's a skill. You learn it. Like you can learn the elements of composition."

"But not how to compose yourself. OK. Show me how to get the material off the computer and how to use the fax and I'm in business."

He looked at her as if not quite believing her cool.

"Oh, my husband needed me to be computer literate, Owen. So I could transfer all his card-index material on to database. And typeset the Coote

Society's magazine. And of course the Internet's a useful research tool. We used Virgin as a provider," she added, deadpan.

He caught her eye, holding it until they were both giggling. "I thought you said you didn't have any skills. You can't get much more marketable than that. You've got to get out of that school, Becky. And out of that cottage."

She nodded briskly. "That's tomorrow's job. Let's get on with tonight's. Let's see — eight o'clock now — is three hours enough?"

"Some of the orchestration may be a bit sketchy . . . OK, avanti!"

He was dimly aware of her working quietly away — certainly not interrupting him with questions. At one point, putting a mug of tea where he could reach it but not knock it over, she asked, "Where's your manual? And the number of your Internet helpline?" No, he wasn't using Virgin.

When he'd shown her, he lost interest. Most of his brain had lost interest, at least. He could hear the murmur of her voice, and the tapping of the computer keys. But then she slipped out of the room again.

"Come in!"

Why should anyone knock his door? Unless Dad was coming in all apologetic, and was heralding a grovel with a bit of formality. Or maybe hot chocolate and biscuits, and he couldn't open the door one-handed. He pulled himself out of bed and opened the door. Hot chocolate and biscuits, yes. Dad, no.

166

"Becky! This is great. Come along in." He remembered how Dad felt about his room. "Watch where you put your feet."

She looked really pissed off. "I suppose there is some system here?" She put down the mug and plate, then stood, hands on hips, staring.

"Be nice if there were. I suppose it's cleans over there, dirties over here."

She grabbed a handful. "Linen basket? So your Mrs Thing knows which to wash?"

He glowered. "Don't you start."

"Get back into bed," she said flatly. "I'm not only starting, I'm finishing. We've got to get you a bag packed for tomorrow. Your dad's too busy, and you're too groggy. But if you take some of these socks — well, I suppose it'd cut down the petrol consumption." She grinned: he was being forgiven.

He laughed. "OK. There should be clean things in the airing cupboard. And my holdall's on the top of the wardrobe."

She popped out, returning with the bathroom linen basket. "Not that it'll do the overall ambience of the bathroom much good, having all these socks ponging away. Tim, you're such a civilised, decent person — what's this problem with clothes?"

He put on a Tony grin. "Everyone needs one imperfection."

She grabbed a handful and rubbed them in his face. "Just to highlight all the other perfections? Great theory, shame about the practice."

It didn't take her long to tidy up.

Be nice to have her there doing it for him again. Be nice to have her around calming Dad down. "None of Dad's other girlfriends has done this," Tim said. "You know, helped Dad, cleaned my room."

"Other girlfriends? I'm not a girlfriend."

He looked at her more closely. "I think he wants you to be. You mustn't be upset he hasn't noticed your new things. When he's composing, Cate Blanchett could drop by and he wouldn't notice."

"And has she ever?"

"Oh, she's a bit young for Dad."

"Tony says you've nearly had some Hollywood stepmothers."

"No. Not really. Dad might have been shagging them, but only because he thought he ought to."

She seemed to freeze, then said, as if she hadn't quite heard, "I'm sorry?"

"Well, if that sort of totty presents itself on a plate, what should a man do? Mind you," he added, "to be fair, he's not brought many home. Wants to set me a good example, I suppose. But you see, all his friends think they ought to marry him off."

"Does he think he should be married off?" She sat at his desk, her back to him, matching clean socks from a pile in her lap.

"Don't know. They do, because of me. They're afraid he's missing out, having to waste time amusing a kid."

"I'm quite sure he doesn't see it that way, Tim. Quite sure," she said, turning to face him. "I was with him yesterday, remember. If ever a man loved his son, Owen loves you."

Her earnestness made him shift in the bed. And he had an idea he'd said a couple of things to upset her.

"You are coming to the bonfire, aren't you? Everyone'll be there!"

"People like these?" She touched some of his photographs. "You took these yourself?"

"Yes. Dad gave me this little camera — really neat. I take it everywhere. And he's got this mate with a darkroom — we develop and print them. The best ones, anyway. What d'you think?" OK, so he was fishing for compliments. But some weren't at all bad.

She looked at them, lingering over a couple of his favourites. "Those are really good. Do you want me to pack the camera, too?"

"It's in the top drawer. Payne-in-the-Arse banned it from school. Hey, do you suppose Dad'll be taking me away and finding somewhere else?"

"What do you think? And what would you prefer?"

"Oh, well, what I'd really like is to live here and go to school in Newton Abbot or Exeter or somewhere. A nice ordinary state school. But — you know Dad. I can't see that happening. Not unless I can persuade him to get a proper housekeeper . . . The T-shirts and sweat-shirts should be in that long drawer." He watched her select a few and shove them in. His head was beginning to throb so he lay down flat again. There was something he needed to know, something she hadn't said . . . "The bonfire," he said, opening his eyes again. "You will be coming, won't you?"

169

She turned away. "I don't know. I shan't know anyone, you see —"

"You'll know the Gayes. They always come. And the Wibley-Wobbly-Webleys."

"What about people from the school?"

"It's the start of half-term. Hardly anyone there. Oh, the masters. But not boys. That's why Dad has it then. He does it for the villagers. And some of his mates. And I suppose with some of his mates there's another reason for not having pretty schoolboys around. And some of his women friends'll be there. Not Cate Blanchett, mind."

"If she's not coming, I couldn't possibly deign to."

"What's up, Becky?" He pulled himself back on to his elbow and, shading his eyes against the bedside light, peered at her.

"Look, Tim, you know what my place is like. You've seen my clothes. How could I possibly show my face? I'd be like Cinderella with no fairy godmother."

"But we all wear jeans and wellies. All of us. And now you've had your hair done — well, get a bit more make-up and you'll be fine. You know, mascara and stuff. And I really want you to come."

"We'll see," she said in the tone of voice his dad had always used when he'd made up his mind and wasn't prepared to argue about it. She looked at her watch. "Come on, Tim, love — go and clean your teeth before you settle down for the night."

"Eh?"

"You've got lovely gnashers. Shame to risk damaging them. And I'll sort out your bed a bit."

He hardly noticed until, grabbing Duck, he turned on his side. She'd stripped everything and put on fresh bedclothes. He'd always liked fresh bedclothes . . .

CHAPTER
TWENTY

"Your e-mail's up and running again," Rebecca said, as Owen looked up.

"Great." He said absently, stretching carefully. There were ominous crunchings from his neck. "Hell, I'm getting too old for crouching over a desk. I shall have to see the vet again." He got up and stretched again. Any moment he should return to the here and now. But for the time being he was locked in nineteenth-century Australia. He drank some tea. Lukewarm. Still, he was used to making tea and forgetting all about it. When had he made this? And then, very slowly, it dawned on him that he hadn't. Rebecca ... "Did you say something about e-mail?"

"I said it was up and running again. I phoned the helpline. I don't know what it's done to your phone bill."

"To hell with the phone bill! You're an angel! Now I can get this stuff on to disk and send it off. I've got this really clever program — I'll show you. Hang on — Tim! Oh, my God." He'd left him on his own all this time. Anything could have happened. And he called himself a father!

"Tim's fine," she said calmly. "He's probably asleep by now."

He was halfway out of the door but stopped in time. "Would you mind if I went and checked?"

"Would I mind!" she laughed. "Off you go."

"I'll only be a minute."

"Sure."

The room must be sound-proofed. No one would hear if she played for a few minutes. The way her fingers would be, she certainly wouldn't want to be heard. She looked through the pile of sheet music on the piano: most of it was far too difficult for her. But there was some Schubert she could tackle. Only schoolgirl stuff. But the luxury of being able to play again, even if it was only the piano. What she'd have loved to do was open the cello case standing in the corner. But the piano was infinitely better than nothing. If only she could make her fingers stretch. If only she could think about something except her pain.

My God, he was back already. Her face on fire, she pushed herself to her feet. "I'm so sorry — I couldn't resist —"

"For God's sake don't apologise." He sounded almost irate. "Not after the transformation you've wrought in Tim's room."

"He tells me it's his only fault." The blush was subsiding, thank goodness.

"Trouble is, he's probably right. But thanks. And presumably it was you who saw to his bag? I wish I didn't have to do this, Becky. I really do. Especially

173

now." He put his hand on her arm. "Especially now." His eyes fixed on hers, dropping to her lips, he slid his hand down to hers.

She couldn't bear it! She couldn't. Not if she were simply one in a line. Hell, of course she'd be one in a line. A man of her age or more! So long as she were the last in the line. Some hope of that. He was just feeling sorry for her.

And don't forget he hadn't wanted her to disgrace him at the bonfire.

Pulling away, she turned from him. Swallowing, she made herself ask, "How does this program work?"

He would be searching her face for some explanation, wouldn't he? Well, her face couldn't give it, not if her head didn't know what it was. All she had to do was see this evening out, and then she could have a period of quiet reflection. Not to want a man to kiss you when your whole body was crying out to have sex with him — no, it didn't make a lot of sense.

Wheeling over to the computer, she pulled up a spare chair.

If only he had more time. Something had really upset her, God knows what. And for Christ's sake, he simply didn't have time to deal with it all out now. An hour and a half to go. If she really had sorted the e-mail business, there was absolutely no problem. He'd have plenty of time to talk to her. Mustn't forget he had to set the alarm for five thirty. Oh, shit and shit and shit.

He sat down. "Here. Here're the stave lines. And you can choose which clefs you want. And the key signature there. The rhythm. Instrumentation. All very nice. But

174

this — this will actually complete the orchestration based on my preferences. My style, if you like."

"So if Brahms had had one of these he could simply have tapped in 'Three Blind Mice' and had it sound like — well, Brahms."

"Absolutely. If not quite as simply as that."

"So all you have to do now is tap in your ms., and it'll transcribe it and orchestrate it and everything."

"That's right. And thanks to you I can e-mail the file. And thanks to the wonders of modern technology, they can actually hear how it sounds as they look at the ms."

"My God." She looked like a child in a toy shop. "Would you mind if I watched?"

How could he say no? Except his fingers would all become thumbs — they always did when anyone watched. "Be my guest." He fetched the ms. and started. Badly. Over and over again. If only he could ask her to go back to the piano — any bloody place but here.

"It's no good, is it?" she said quietly. "You're using the delete button enough to wear it out. I'll go and make another pot of tea, shall I?"

"This time of night better make it herbal tea," he said. "In the cupboard nearest the kettle."

But it wasn't being watched that had made him fumble. Not entirely, anyway. It was having her beside him, knowing something had upset her, knowing she'd made a supreme effort in everything he'd asked of her and not being able to put right whatever wrong she'd been done. A woman like that didn't simply get so uptight because you didn't notice her clothes, surely?

Anyway, if he rattled along now, he'd have time to make some sort of recompense. Provided bloody Tony didn't take it into his head to show up!

She had half a mind simply to slip away. She had her bike, after all. But that didn't seem very grown up. She could take his tea through and say a polite goodnight. That would be best. But that would mean depriving herself of the painful pleasure of watching those long strong fingers move across even such a prosaic thing as a computer keyboard. Imagine watching him play the piano. That profile, those hands — *Stop it! You're behaving like a lovelorn teenager!*

So what sort of tea would he want? There was quite a selection of teabags. She put some at random on a plate, filled two mugs with boiling water — why two, Rebecca? — and carried the tray through.

"Galloping along," he said over his shoulder. "Just to be on the safe side, let's save it before I drink — hot water?"

"Dunk your own," she said, passing the plate.

He looked at her until it became uncomfortable and she turned away. "Did your late husband expect you to be Wonderwoman, Becky?"

"Expect! Demand, more like. I'm not Wonderwoman, Owen, you know that. It's just that if I made mistakes, I regretted it. He never hit me. Don't think that. But you know when you hear of those women who've been assaulted by their men, and you wonder why they put up with it — well, I suppose that's how it was with Rupert. I did my best — well, that was the way I was brought up! — with everything. But if there was a slip he'd lacerate me with his tongue. Lacerate." She turned away. He mustn't start being kind, not like the Gayes. Or she'd cry again, and she knew she couldn't trust herself if he tried to comfort her. Lower lip still between her teeth, she turned back.

As if trying to lighten her load, Owen said, "But you weren't always Rebecca Wildbore — oh, Becky, what a name. Was he?" His fingers described imaginary tusks.

She laughed. Not just to please him. "It depends how you put the stresses on his name, I suppose. And many might simply have found him terribly tedious. No, I was plain Rebecca Hughes when he married me."

"I shouldn't think you were ever plain. Now your hair's shorter, you're — you're —"

She grabbed a tuft. "It's not what I wanted. But it'll grow again."

"Yes — they should have left it longer at the back. But —" He touched her cheek, following the line of the bones.

She flushed. If only he wouldn't. If only . . .

"Rebecca Hughes . . . I have a feeling I ought to know the name."

"Can't think why," she said shortly.

"You never went to the Royal Academy?"

"My niece did. And my cello."

"You play the cello! Why didn't you try Tim's?" He was across the room and opening the cello case.

"No. You know as well as I do that you don't even touch anyone's musical instrument without their permission," she said sharply. Though she sank to her knees to look at this. Couldn't resist.

"You know as well as I do that Tim would want you to play it. Why did you let your own go?"

"Because my niece is talented, because Rupert hated to hear me practise, because I became simply a curiosity tucked away in the university orchestra, because — well, I could hardly have brought it to the cottage, could I?"

"You didn't know about the cottage. Becky — why?"

"I've only lent it to her."

"That's no answer."

"What does it matter?" And why was he so insistent? She was so out of her depth she wished she'd escaped earlier. She turned sharply from him.

He let it go. But she could hear him writing. He was folding paper, shoving it in his pocket. Now he was going back to the computer, and starting to tap once again. So why didn't she go home?

All done. All done. Thanks to this crazy edgy woman. However much he wanted her, he couldn't pursue her any more. Not tonight. For both their sakes he had to leave it. There was stuff in her past, more recent stuff, too, that had to be worked through. All he knew now was that he had to be up horribly early and drive Tim safely to London. It was always like this. All the energy he needed when he was working. Then nothing.

As for her, there she was head down on the piano, fast asleep. She looked as young and fragile as Tim. Especially in that T-shirt. It'd be a nice gesture, while she slept, to iron her top, that pretty one he'd never complimented her on.

178

He tiptoed from the room, heading for the utility room. What neither of them had noticed was the label inside the top. DRY CLEAN ONLY. Silly kid, buying something as impractical as that. Yet it might iron. He'd risk it. And he'd have to find some way of making up this horrible evening to her.

Well, the blouse didn't come up too badly: he'd always prided himself on being better at ironing than the average Mrs Thing, though he did have to admit the present one was a real expert. He slipped it into a carrier which he hung by her coat.

She was still asleep when he slipped back into the music room, her head and neck so vulnerable now the hair was shorn. And he wondered what it would be like to have this head next to his on the pillow. Whenever he woke. Wherever he woke.

CHAPTER
TWENTY-ONE

Rebecca awoke with a start. Owen had his hand on her shoulder and was laughing down at her. His voice was very gentle.

"Poor Becky. I'm afraid between them the Griffithses have worn you out."

God! Had she been snoring? Dribbling? She staggered to her feet.

"No hurry." His face was concerned. "Look — I —"

"I'd better be getting back, hadn't I?"

"There's no hurry, surely." Was he saying that for politeness' sake? Impossible to tell. He certainly looked drained, and no wonder after the last thirty-six hours.

"You've got to be up and away pretty early, haven't you? So why don't I just bowl off now?" Her voice sounded remarkably sensible. Horribly sensible.

"You're bowling nowhere on your own at this time of night. I'm sure your bike'll fit into the dowager-mobile. But you're more than welcome to stay . . . I mean, if — if you wanted. The spare bed — it's always . . ."

For a moment she thought he wanted her to. And not in the spare bed either. And perhaps it wouldn't be ignominious to follow Meryl Streep or whoever. But

180

whatever his eyes were saying, his voice was being as sensible as hers.

"It'd be less nuisance now than in the morning," she said with care. "And if I'm here Tim'll only start protesting again."

"I'm afraid you're right." She could have sworn he suppressed a sigh of relief. "He's always been such an amenable kid. I suppose he's going to get stroppier and stroppier."

"I'm sure he'll rejoin the human race sooner than most. I hope so."

They'd drifted into the hall. He bent to pick up a carrier, presenting it to her with a courtly bow. "Your top, Ms Hughes. I'm afraid it may be totally buggered. Should have been dry cleaned."

Oh, no. All that money down the drain and she'd never even had the sense to read the label!

"However, you had the nous to wash it in cold water, and I'm a dab hand with the steam iron. Maybe it'll live. And if it doesn't, my insurance policy will pay for it. Understood?"

Oh, yes, this was kindness. He knew, didn't he, she wouldn't let him pay for it himself.

"Understood. Thanks." She smiled, shyly.

"When I'm working like this everything goes out of my head. Including the things I want to say. Like how nice you looked in the top. And how your hair shines. And how good you look in that jacket. You stay here in the warm — I'll bring the car round."

"Owen."

"Yes?"

"Might I just have one more look at Tim? I won't wake him."

"I'll come up with you."

Tim slept like a baby, his mouth slightly open. A yellow duckling was just visible under his hand.

It had taken both of them to manoeuvre the old bike into the Volvo, but they managed it. They were laughing about it all the way down his drive. And it was easy to pick up his light tone about London traffic and Tim's grandmother and the work he'd be doing in London. But, once he'd parked outside her cottage, it didn't seem easy for either of them to say goodbye.

"You will look after yourself?" he was saying with such earnestness.

"Of course. I'll be quite busy. First read-through of *Hamlet* on Saturday."

"I thought it was supposed to be all-male."

"They can slum when it comes to the prompter."

He threw his head back and laughed. But then he was serious again. "And there's the Autumn Fair on Saturday afternoon. Make sure you go — it's the best way to meet the villagers. Once they take to you, you're theirs for life."

"I did think of starting on my paintwork."

"Not until after the fair. Go for the homemade tomato chutney. In fact, I'll commission you to buy me some. And some jam. As much as you can carry. Here." He dug in his back pocket, producing a couple of folded notes.

"No, it doesn't matter."

"Becky, you know full well it does. You haven't mentioned being paid yet. So I gather Clifford-Payne pays well in arrears."

"His name's actually Payne, you know. He hyphenated his first name to it about twelve years ago. Anyway, I'm sure you're right about pay. So thank you." She slipped the money into her handbag.

He looked at it disapprovingly. "If I drive a dowagermobile, that's awfully close to a dowager's bag. More Queen Mother-style, actually. There's a man comes down to the fair every year with hand-crafted bags. Shoulder bags. Another commission. Get one from me."

"No!"

"Don't tell me no. You worked your socks off tonight and I'll find some way to thank you if it kills me." Still laughing, he dropped his voice. "Someone is watching us from the hedge over there. Don't look up. Don't move. Any moment now I'm going to run like the devil and try and catch him. Use that if I get him." He slipped a mobile phone into her lap.

If he thought she was going to be a passive onlooker when he was running hell for leather across the road, he was mistaken. She was on his heels, ready to help. But they lost him. They heard the crash of undergrowth further down the hill, but even that went quiet.

"We'll get the bike under cover. Then I'm going to check out that cottage, phone the police, and lock you in. OK?"

"Fine."

"Right," Owen said, a few minutes later. "You're as safe as you can be. But I want you to take this. And carry it everywhere — even in the Queen Mother's handbag — and use it. Promise?"

"What'll you use?"

"Didn't you notice the hands-free one in the car? And I'm not a woman on my own. With a peeping Tom in the neighbourhood."

She didn't argue. "You'll phone — to let me know how Tim's getting on?"

"Of course. If anything does go wrong — but it won't! — a private car will collect you. I'm not joking. But nothing will go wrong. The bugger of it is I'm probably being wildly overcautious, and he'd have been fine with you and Mrs Thing. Well, there never was any doubt about him being fine with you. I'm sorry. I seem to have messed everything up. This was the last thing I wanted to be doing this weekend. And as for this evening, I've screwed that up in every way possible."

No one had ever dropped his voice like that to speak to her, looked at her with eyes that pleaded.

If only she could say something. Anything. That it didn't matter if one evening was a mess, so long as there could be others. All she could do was smile. And reach for him to kiss her. Which he did, with infinite tenderness. But no, not with passion.

CHAPTER
TWENTY-TWO

Rebecca's day started with a short and businesslike call from Owen, at a motorway service station, he said.

"I forgot to tell you," he said, "how to switch that mobile off — you don't want loads of calls for me. And Tim tells me there's a way we can page between my car mobile and the one you've got. He did explain — but you know what I'm like with technology."

"How is Tim?"

"Oh, he sends his love, of course — but he's too busy with some damned games machine to tell you himself. Or too embarrassed. He seems to have become a proper teenager almost overnight."

"That's what happens if you get a bang on the head!"

"You don't suppose if I banged the other side he'd become my nice kid again?"

"So long as you only do it within spitting distance of a hospital."

"Or sicking distance. Your carpet — is it — all right?"

"Owen, nothing will ever make my carpet all right. Tim's sick is just one more scribble on a pretty nasty palimpsest."

He shouted with laughter.

Yes, it was so easy when they weren't together, when she wasn't worrying about messy hair, or overpriced clothes.

"I've run out of change. Talk to you soon as I can," he said. "And, Becky — look after yourself." His voice sounded intimate, yes, tender. And was cut off abruptly.

By rights it should have been another wonderfully sunny morning. In fact it was beginning to rain quite sharply, and Rebecca could see no good reason for getting soaked in the course of a long walk when she had a perfectly good bike at her disposal. Bother Clifford and his stupid injunction. But — though she would cycle to the nearest job centre as soon as she had a chance — at the moment she needed this job. And Clifford, if truly annoyed, could probably find some way of denying her even the pittance she'd earned over the last few days. And would throw her out of the cottage. Owen? Could he really provide a refuge? He'd more or less offered. But — oh, if even in a fairytale world he did want a relationship with her — she would want to go to him by mutual choice, not because she needed shelter. It had to be choice. On both their parts. And what about Tim's feelings? In the cold — and wet — light of day, she knew that Tim and Owen had even more to lose if their relationship went sour than she had.

God, Becky was taking risks, wasn't she? Cycling up the drive in the broad light of day, wearing trousers. Well, rumour had it that the old man had told her not to wear a skirt to cycle in. And she probably wouldn't know about all the kerfuffle when the Webley woman insisted on wearing leggings to work. He'd have to have a word with her fast. The moment assembly was over, in fact.

Shit! There was no sign of her in the library when he arrived. Plenty of other people, though. It'd really help her case if his bloody father came hunting for her and found a riot. No. No riot. Not with old Sowerby standing there flicking through the *Guardian* and peering over his specs every few minutes. He'd got a bit of a soft spot for her, hadn't he? Handing over the bike like that. And — Jesus Christ! — it looked as if someone else had a soft spot, too. Soft enough to give her roses. It could be the colour of the roses that made her look as if she were blushing, carrying them in an ugly art room vase along the corridor. He'd bet it was a genuine blush. And he'd bet he knew who'd sent the roses.

"Owen been saying thank you, then?" he asked, lounging over casually, nodding at Sowerby *en route*.

"There was no need," she said. "Anyone would have done the same." But she slipped the card into her skirt pocket. "Oh, Tony, I've got a message for you. From Owen, as it happens. About Sunday lunch." She explained.

"I'd have thought you'd be the obvious person to keep an eye on Tim," Tony said.

"I'm working here, aren't I? Your invaluable librarian."

"Not for much longer if the Chief Master sees you wearing jeans."

"Am I wearing jeans? I see no jeans!" She covered one eye and closed the other. "I do, on the other hand, see Mr Swain approaching, starboard side. Thank you, Payne," she added loudly.

Well, she was learning, wasn't she? He had to hand it to her. She'd come on a bundle since she'd arrived. Which no doubt meant she wouldn't be staying here long. What would the place be like without her? He didn't want to think about it. Amazing what a difference a couple of weeks could make.

"I'm absolutely convinced the library should have computers," Becky was saying.

The male heads nodded: Sowerby; Cavendish; the bursar; Clifford. She was sure that they'd invited her to the meeting in the bursar's room largely because they wanted someone to pour the tea, but possibly because Sowerby — or perhaps Cavendish — had remarked that to have a meeting about the library without the librarian might be unusual.

She'd poured the tea all right, but was not going to sit there silent and not very decorative.

"After all," she continued, "higher education expects its students to be able to type their assignments. You're disadvantaging your young men if we send them off used to producing scruffy, handwritten work. And — with all due respect to my predecessor — there aren't many reference books."

"Books full-stop," Cavendish muttered.

"Given the price of books these days, it might just be cheaper to buy CD-roms. Of course, the initial outlay would be quite high, but if we bought the right hardware and software, we could have our pupils surfing the net just like school children all over the country."

"It would look good in the brochures, Chief Master," Cavendish said.

"I would go further, Chief Master. It will be disastrous for recruitment if we can't put it in the brochure." Sowerby looked around.

No one spoke against. The day was theirs.

Sowerby was speaking again. "While we're here, Chief Master, I would like to bring to your attention a petition which some of the boys have been circulating. I made it clear when I intercepted it that they should have made a direct and polite request to you. But these are the days of pressure groups, so what can we expect?"

"Petition?" Poor Clifford had been trying for some seconds to make a sharp interjection, but once Sowerby embarked on one of his pseudo-Payne utterances, no one would find it easy to interrupt.

"Concerning the library opening hours, Chief Master. The boys want alterations, indeed extensions. But that would involve Mrs Wildbore in making changes to her working pattern, and it seemed to me vital that we should have her views. Now, what the boys want is to be able to use the library at lunchtime and after school. They say — and I can scarcely disagree — that it is a waste of resources to have it open during assembly, for instance. And during lunch itself."

189

"How many hours would this be in total?" the bursar asked, his pencil poised.

"If we include a short period on Saturday afternoon and another on Sunday afternoon, almost fifty hours."

The bursar jotted, and muttered sharply to Clifford.

Fifty hours! Reg might have thought he was being kind, but those hours wouldn't suit her at all. Every day of the week! It would be nice to have the security of a full-time job, but at that cost! She caught herself up: what she wanted was to reserve some time in case — oh, yes, in case . . .

She said firmly, "If we're introducing IT into the library, and improving the opening hours, it's clear you'll need more staff."

"I beg your pardon, Mrs Wildbore?" Clifford looked as amazed as if the table had spoken.

"The introduction of IT — plus, I hope, a much larger book and periodical budget — means at least two staff on duty at busy times." That would solve the problem of the weekend shifts — they could be rotated.

If only she had someone to share it all with. Clifford and the bursar staring at her as if she'd suddenly grown another head; Sowerby clearly enjoying everything; Cavendish looking disconcerted, to say the least. That surprised her: if he'd admired her enough to set up the Monday evening celebration, he must have expected her to have original ideas from time to time.

But there was no one. Not at the moment. If she admitted to herself just how much she longed for Owen to call her, she might lose her buzz. As it was, she must feed herself and then perhaps do some washing.

190

Tomorrow morning, after all, was going to be busy, and Owen had been quite adamant about her going to the fair. Besides which, despite the rain, what she hung in the outhouse should be dry enough to iron tomorrow evening. Yes, busy-busy, that was the answer. No hoping, certainly no longing. Just keeping the mind and the hands busy. She could even listen to the radio, in the hope she could pick up some music between the hisses and spits.

As they sat in what was grandly called the Drama Studio and had probably once been a pleasant breakfast room, facing as it did the morning sun, Rebecca knew she had made a mistake. An extremely tedious, time-consuming mistake. She'd blithely expected this Saturday morning session to last perhaps two hours, three at most. Now it seemed that Mr Cowley wanted the cast to read through the entire play. Since he hadn't yet decided which cuts to make, and since he expected her to note them as he went along, it would take at least four hours. More, if he couldn't get things organised more quickly. He certainly wasn't very well. This morning, his voice was hoarse and he kept feeling his throat. But he should have prepared ahead better than this. At last, she coughed — she'd meant to sound apologetic but everyone's head turned in her direction as if she were being authoritative. "Mr Cowley. I'm very much afraid that these young men will miss their lunch. Perhaps we could just concentrate on the opening — after all, so many of the leads are off playing rugby, aren't they? And I have to leave at one."

191

I have to leave at one. She could see the words being savoured by the boys. The silence, whether shocked or appreciative, lengthened. Should she soften what she'd said by suggesting his voice had done enough? On the whole she thought not.

At last Cowley opened his mouth. And smiled, if gravely. "A timely warning, Mrs Wildbore. I'm afraid we thespians do get carried away."

If he could be courteous, so could she. "But when thespians have bad throats they should look after them," she smiled.

He nodded. "Well, Francisco, well, Barnardo: stand not upon the order of your going!"

They didn't. Neither did the others. And old Cowley was kind enough to offer her a lift back to her cottage. Her moment's fear — what if he drove like his wife? — wasn't, she was glad to say, justified.

CHAPTER
TWENTY-THREE

Becky got back to the cottage to find an Interflora card through the front door. *Flowers round back*, it said. More roses. This time, the note said, *Just to remind you about my commissions*.

This was crazy, crazy. No one had ever sent her flowers before. Ever. And not roses whose scent was so sensuous you could have bathed in it. In fact, she buried her face in them, coming up for air as if the top of her head would blow off.

So what could she put them in? A vase, in a cottage like this? For the time being she stowed them in the plastic bucket that had once held the shallots. She'd see what she could pick up at the fair this afternoon. If it was anything like the ones she'd been to in Radnorshire when she was young, hideous was likely to be the order of the day. Still, she could always ask Mrs Gaye to lend a vase to her.

She was just setting out, Owen's money stashed deep in a pocket, when on impulse she popped back. Two jars of pickled shallots. OK, rather small jars. They all were. But she was sure there'd be some stall that would welcome a donation. She slipped them into a plastic carrier.

The rain had given way to bright sunshine and a gusty wind. She felt like a kid, desperate to stretch her arms and pretend to fly into it. Just as Jack was doing. When she called Tamsin turned and waited for her, pushing a dummy back into Rosie's mouth.

"Such a bore. Still, *noblesse oblige*, I suppose," Tamsin said. "Got to humour the yokels, us incomers, haven't we?"

She ought to say something firm. People like the Gayes didn't deserve to be patronised, not by someone who gave rotting shallots as a thank-you present for saving a baby's life. But before she could speak, Jack fell flat, and started to howl.

"Goodness, you cry baby. Come on, let's look. No, no blood. Oh, do shut up. Or no treats for you. God, the joys of parenthood. I wonder who'll be there this afternoon."

"Are you expecting anyone?" Rebecca hitched Jack up on to her hip, rubbing his knee.

"No. Not unless his nibs brings some of his famous chums. Hey, didn't I hear that you saved young Tim's life or something? Oh, I suppose these things always get exaggerated, don't they? In a village like this. So what do you think of him?"

"I think he's one of the nicest kids I've ever met," Becky replied, enjoying being perverse. "Really charming. And kind." She returned Jack to terra firma.

Tamsin gave Jack another shake. "Hear that, Jack? Rebecca likes young Tim. He doesn't walk along the road grizzling all the time." She turned to Becky again. "No, not him. His dad. Owen."

"I didn't see much of him." She was just about to add that he'd been busy working. But Tamsin probably knew nothing of yesterday evening: it had better stay that way. "He was the patient's father. I just tagged along."

"Don't suppose he even thanked you."

"He sent me some lovely flowers," Becky said. Tamsin would hear that from the grapevine soon enough.

"Such a snob. Keeps himself to himself. Says he's busy. And of course, he keeps dashing off to the States or wherever. Meeting all those glamorous people — no wonder he can't be bothered with the likes of us. But the least he could have done was open the fair, don't you think? After all, it's for the church roof."

"I gathered he wasn't going to be in Devon today."

"Oh, off jet-setting again." She continued, apparently in the same breath, "I hear you're seeing a lot of young Tony."

Rebecca stopped short. What on earth could you say to something like that? But Tamsin didn't need a prompt. "Gorgeous, isn't he? You wonder how on earth anyone like Payne-in-the-Arse could have fathered him. Hmm, makes me feel like the Wife of Bath, just thinking about him."

They were approaching the stalls. If Rebecca were going to be able to hand over the shallots without causing offence, then she had to split from Tamsin. And split very delicately, if she didn't want to be bad-mouthed. But everyone was gathering in a knot to hear the opening speech. No, not from Owen, of course. Even she recognised that face from the TV.

Jack was whining again, and Tamsin busy shushing him, so Rebecca missed his opening words. But he continued, ". . . opened by my old friend Owen Griffiths. But he's got one of these sudden urges — you know what these creative people are like . . . a symphony here, a concerto there! So he asked me to come instead. He also asked me to tell you that young Tim is just fine — I'm sure you'll all know his son was hurt in an accident the other day. I gather it was one of you good people who saved his life. Bless you, whoever it was. Tim's a darling boy and we'd have hated anything to happen to him, wouldn't we?"

Pause for loud murmur of assent. Several people turned to look at Rebecca, making little gestures of silent applause. She wished the ground would open.

"Now, what you've all got to do is save this church. I've got a cheque here from Owen, Vicar," — he flapped it round till the Vicar took it — "and another from little me. What you've got to do is dig in your pockets like you've dug in your gardens . . ."

"I bet his fee's a damned sight bigger than the cheque," Tamsin said aloud. "Oh, do get on with it, we're all freezing."

If the Personality heard, he gave no sign. But he declared the fair open, and set off, at a very brisk pace, with an entourage comprising the Vicar, the Vicar's wife and a grey-haired woman Rebecca wouldn't identify but who looked a fair organiser if anyone did. He zipped round all the stalls, flashing his wallet and

196

acquiring all sorts of unlikely things. And then he was into a Jaguar and on his way. Chauffeur-driven.

"Just like bloody royalty," Tamsin observed. "Now, I suppose we'd better buy some rubbish or other."

"I'll catch you later," Rebecca said. "I think Mrs Gaye wants me."

She went via the bottle stall, intending simply to slip the jars to the woman running it. She'd no idea who she was. But as she fished them from the bag, the Vicar materialised by her side. He looked very tired. "Mrs Wildbore, isn't it? Mike Green."

She smiled. "Rebecca."

They shook hands.

"I was just . . ." she gestured with the jars. "Rather a widow's mite, I'm afraid."

He smiled gently, "If you have nothing, something is a great deal. Heavens! That sounded pretty aphoristic, didn't it. I must write that down. Recycle it in a sermon. You won't tell anyone, will you?"

"If you promise not to reveal who you said it to."

He touched his nose like a conspirator. "It'd be nice if you joined our flock regularly, Rebecca."

"God and I — haven't been on speaking terms."

"I gather you've had some very trying years. Try having a word with Him now. His line's usually open. Ah! My wife — Carrie, have you met Rebecca . . ."

The stall she wanted most was the leather-worker's. She didn't want to run out of the money she knew he wanted her to use to buy that bag. Equally, she didn't want to fail in her mission to buy jam and pickles for

197

Owen. It was like being a child again, as if she had coins clutched hot in her hand, and her mother had told her not spend on sweets until she'd bought the things on her list. Why not use the childhood ruse — check out the price of what she really wanted, and then zap round spending the rest. And she wanted a vase, too. That was easy. Her money. What little she had.

Leather bags. She'd never had a leather bag, so she had no idea whether these were good value or not. What she did know was that they represented at least three weeks' food. She could even have worked out exactly many hours' toil she'd have to put in at Low Ash to pay for them.

Her impulse — all those years' training — was to buy the cheapest. No, Owen wouldn't want that. But she had an idea that he wouldn't want her simply to chose the most expensive, either. He'd want her to have the one she liked best.

The choice was agony. Stupid, stupid agony. All the time she hesitated, jam and pickles were being sold, and she might fail him.

The man must have been getting irritated by her indecision. She was getting irritated by her indecision. At last, she pointed and that was it. Bag bought. Money handed over. And the world hadn't ended.

Neither had the jam run out. Nor the pickles. She bought ten pounds' worth of each. Well, that was what Owen had wanted. And then, daring as if she were buying caviar, she bought a couple of jars for herself. If only she'd brought a proper shopping-bag — the handles of the plastic carrier were straining badly under the load. How long her fingers would cope was another matter.

"You want to leave that over at the tombola," Mr Gaye called. "With Mary. No, of course she won't mind. Go on, then you can enjoy yourself — come and roll for a pig."

Well, whatever she could do with a pig she didn't know. But she'd come back as soon as she'd stowed her bag with Mrs Gaye.

"You been spending your money, my dear," she observed, tucking it under the skirt of the stall.

"Owen's money, actually."

"Ah, he's a nice lad. Now, ten pence a go. See what you win." She spun the tombola.

A bottle of bubbles! The sort you blew through a wand. She'd not done that since she was a child!

"Oh, what a shame. There's some proper bubbly here — have another go."

Rebecca checked her change. "Not if I'm going to win a pig!" And somehow, bubbles were just what she wanted to fill her cottage with this evening. Even if they did burst.

The bric-à-brac stall next. For a vase.

"You're never going to buy *that*!"

"Hello, Tamsin. Had a good shop?"

"All this pathetic tat. And people rooting round like it's *Antiques Roadshow*. Ah, well, no accounting for taste."

No, indeed.

"Mind you, I'd still say that that would be more at home in a graveyard than in a house. Your money, though."

A whole fifty pence.

"Right, I'm going to win a pig next," Rebecca said, clutching the vase. "Are you coming to watch, Jack?"

"Balloon," he said.

Well, he would, wouldn't he? But they weren't just ordinary balloons, they were the sort you were supposed to let go so that they flew for miles. The winner would get — what, a crate of wine? Jack would do well with that. And they cost fifty pence each. If she bought him a balloon it meant no pig. And Tamsin was clearly waiting for her to cough up. That was what people did for children — gave them little presents. She dug frantically in her jeans. There was a little change left over from Owen's jam.

"You're supposed to wish and let go, young man," the balloonman said.

"I don't think he'll like the letting-go part," Becky said. "Tell you what, I'll wish and he can have it tied on to his wrist."

Something must have gone wrong because she could hear Jack's wails even as she handed over Owen's money. Perhaps if she dashed across and handed over the bubble mixture . . . No. She would blow bubbles this evening in her living-room. Jack was Tamsin's problem.

"Is the pig alive or dead?" she asked.

"Either. We can keep it going a bit longer for you — provided you pay its rent, like. Or we can butcher it for your freezer. Go on, you've got a lucky face."

Had she? Well, perhaps she'd have to settle for the wish-filled balloon, hurtling over Dartmoor from Jack's hand. Because her luck had run out, and so had her money.

"So you're seeing young Owen, are you?" Mrs Gaye asked, handing over the bag. "No, I don't like the look of those handles. They'll break and there where will you be? Now, I'm sure I saw a box somewhere — yes, there you are. You put everything in there and George'll drop it by for you. No, don't you argue, silly girl. Now, that *is* a nice bag."

Rebecca found herself blushing. A woman as poor as she clearly was, lashing out on such an extravagance.

"Owen told me he'd told you to get one. Didn't quite say I was to check up. But — yes, that's a nice bag. You could do well with him, my dear."

The blush hurt.

"He's a decent man, young Owen. Real decent. That gentleman that opened the fair — I know what fee he usually asks, and there was no mention of it today. I reckon Owen put his hand in his pocket so we wouldn't have to. Mind you, he might have felt he was letting us down. Which in a way he did. Not like him. But what's-his-name there brought in a lot more people, so there you are."

"Does Owen have a lot of friends like that?"

"Some. Well, it's his world, isn't it? It's real funny, he brings these people into my shop and last time I saw them it was on the big screen. Funny thing, it must be lighting or make-up or something. They're never as nice looking close to. But real friendly. You'd like them."

"Mrs Gaye — I — I'm not in their league!"

"Silly girl, do you think I am? But they've never had any side. Now, I know what you're going to say. You're going to say it's one thing being nice to an old woman in a shop, another being nice to a young woman popped up from nowhere and going out with a man you've known for years. Well, that's true. And some may even say you're after him for his money, but he'd put them right on that."

Rebecca managed a smile. "But he's had all these glamorous girlfriends. And whatever I am, I'm not glamorous."

"True. But it doesn't take glamour to save Tim's life."

"That's another thing. What if he only likes me because he's grateful?"

Mrs Gaye spun the tombola for another customer, who went off with a bottle of sherry. "He didn't talk to me as if he was just grateful." She shifted her balance. "Now, I don't know if I should tell you this, but I'm going to. I said to him on the phone this morning, "She's not like one of your film-star women. I don't want her hurt. If you think this is a flash in the pan, you stay out of her life before she falls for you. She's not someone you take to bed and drop. She's been hurt too bad in the past for that." That's what I said."

She felt as if someone had kicked her stomach. "D'you think that's why he's gone off to London? Because he doesn't want to hurt me?"

Mrs Gaye stood arms akimbo and laughed. "Would a man who didn't want to get involved send you all those roses?"

"But when did you talk?"

"Over the phone this morning, my dear. Like I said. When he was fixing for his friend to come and do the necessary." She snipped an imaginary tape with her fingers. "Come, my dear. I reckon those years with that dreadful man of yours must have done something strange to your head. Well, imagine coming here thinking you might like to marry Mr Clifford-Payne. Come on, sweetheart — is there anyone home there?" She leaned over and lightly tapped Rebecca's forehead. "Now, what's that man of mine saying?"

No one had won the pig, that was what he was saying. And wouldn't Becky like to have one last go? Specially as he'd just found a pound coin lying in the grass.

"You win that, it'd barbecue lovely for the fireworks party," Mrs Gaye said. "You go on. I'll look after this lot. Two goes, remember, for a pound."

CHAPTER
TWENTY-FOUR

Emerging from the church, Tony stared. What on earth was the matter with Becky? The woman was walking like a constipated penguin. Soon as he could, soon as they'd all finished yammering, he'd push his way across and find out. At least she seemed to be hanging around this morning. Not like last week, when she'd scuttled off without waiting to talk to anyone. Ah, she was on her own now. Not that the Gayes would have minded him pushing in anyway.

"What the hell's up with you?" he demanded.

"Hi, Tony. Nice to see you, too." So she was into irony, was she? "Hey, how did you get on in the rugby yesterday? How on earth are you going to combine rugger and *Hamlet*?"

He leaned close to her. "Shut up. Just shut the fuck up," he whispered.

She flinched, and then winced. So even that tiny movement must hurt.

"You'd better come over here." He took her, not roughly, by the arm, and steered her across the graves through the little knots of villagers to Ted Tregannon.

"One for you, Ted, mate," he said without preamble.

Ted hardly paused in what he was saying, but looked her up and down and said, "So I see. How's the knee, Tony?"

"Oh, fine."

"How fine?" Ted pursued, looking over his glasses. "Drop by after surgery tomorrow if you can manage it."

Poor Becky was looking completely lost. She did lost very well. In fact, she could do lost for England. Now, either Ted would take pity on her or he'd be scathing. You never knew with Ted. The best thing to do was leave them to it. Especially with Old Bastard bearing down on him.

"See you," he said, flapping his hand.

"Hang on, young man. How d'you expect me to treat someone I've not been introduced to? Don't they teach you any manners at that school of yours?"

Bloody hell. "Becky. This is Ted Tregannon, the village vet. Ted, I'd like you to meet the new Low Ash librarian, Rebecca Wildbore."

They shook hands. "So you'd like me to get that disc of yours back into place," he said. "OK. I'll sort that before lunch. You stick with us. Ah, morning, Payne."

The OB managed a thin smile — Ted was one of the few people who refused to acknowledge the OB's spurious hyphen. "Good morning — Tregannon. Mrs Tregannon. My dear Mrs Wildbore."

Funny how the OB could make the endearment sound more like a threat.

"Now, I am about to drive back to school, my dear, and thought to offer you a lift. And perhaps a pre-luncheon sherry."

Pre-luncheon sherry and no luncheon, that would be Tony's bet.

Rebecca shook her head minutely and winced again.

"Mrs — what did you say your name was? Becky? Becky'll be coming with me and Tessa, Payne. Look at her," Ted said.

"She looks very charming to me."

"For goodness' sake, look at the angle of her shoulder and back, man."

"I always understood a silk scarf would assist in such cases. Warmth. Mrs Wildbore?" He only offered her his arm, as if they were in some TV costume drama.

"For crying out loud. Becky, get yourself into the Range Rover over there." Ted passed her his keys. "Tessa, you go and see to her, will you?"

"The man's not qualified, Mrs Wildbore."

And suddenly Becky smiled. "That makes two of us, doesn't it, Clifford?" And she turned with Tessa Tregannon, and walked slowly away. Whatever had happened to her? No apology — he'd have expected her to be hesitating and demurring all over the place. Just a simple acceptance. Was she gaining confidence and assurance from somewhere? Or was she simply in a lot of pain?

At least a lot of Payne wasn't in her. But suddenly that wasn't a joke. Even a private one. He had this dreadful image of the OB humping her. His father's broad white back and flabby buttocks; Becky's legs spread wide by the weight. His gross grunting. Her screams.

206

Except it wasn't poor Becky, was it? It must have been something he'd seen as a kid. Mum. He'd seen his father raping her. Jesus. He threw himself towards a tomb-stone just in time for it to hide his vomiting.

He'd have to pass it off somehow. At least now the OB wouldn't press him to accept a lift home — not if he thought he might spew in the new car.

Rebecca waited on her own in the Tregannons' sitting-room. Tessa had sat her down, offering the *Observer* and promising coffee. She could smell the coffee already — fifteen years with no good coffees and now two in one week! — but the conversation in the kitchen was distracting her from the headlines.

She'd no idea what to make of Tregannon. But he must be the vet Owen had mentioned a couple of times. If Owen trusted him he must be all right. Mustn't he? But she could hear his voice raised in apparent anger in the kitchen. If it was irritation that Tony had wished her on him at an inconvenient time, then she'd drink her coffee, make her apologies and go. Pain or not. Well, with her head already tipped to one side, like a bird listening for a worm, she might as well listen.

". . . exaggerating as usual." That was Tessa.

". . . never exaggerate . . . things like this . . ." Ted.

"Just because you don't like him."

"No one in their right mind likes him." As he got more impassioned, it became all too easy to hear him. "Power-mad tinpot despot. But I tell you it was evil. Capital E."

Tessa murmured something.

"Of course there's such a thing as evil. And that's what Payne had in his eye today. Looking at Tony's waif or stray."

Another murmur.

And a concluding rumble.

Evil? Clifford? It didn't make sense? He was a boor and a bully — but evil? She was inclined to agree with Tessa that he was exaggerating. As for herself — well, how else would she describe herself?

If only it could be as Owen's lover.

Perhaps he'd been too busy to phone last night. Perhaps he'd tried to phone while she was at church . . .

"Not that your whole back isn't a mess," Ted said, as part of it crunched back into place. "There. Got you, you little bleeder."

Her shoulder was harpooned with pain. Then it went, as if wiped away. Now he was working on her neck.

"Looks as if you heave coal for a hobby. What have you been doing?"

"I bought a bike," Becky ventured.

"That'd do you nothing but good. If you bothered to get the saddle to the right height. And?"

"A bit of decorating. With a roller."

"On a ladder? Were you high enough?"

"One step — it was a step-ladder — was missing. So I had to stretch a bit."

"When was that?"

"Yesterday evening. After I bowled for a pig."

Ted shook his head. "You've been messing that back around a long time."

"How about eight hours a day on a computer?" she asked.

"Eight hours? I hope your employer allowed you proper rest periods?"

"Hardly," she said. "But it's too late to sue now . . ."

Now the pain was no more than a dull background throb, she could look around her and join in the conversation, such as it was. And tuck into excellent lamb, with wonderful crisp potatoes roasted alongside it, courgettes cooked with garlic and buttered carrots. Even the mint was from the garden, Tessa had said, though she'd claimed she'd have a hard job to find enough at this time of the year.

"You might as well stay," Ted had said roughly. "Tess can't get it into her skull that the kids have flit the coop. And it's too good to throw away. Isn't it, Tess?" he laid his hand over his wife's.

The two exchanged a look Becky wasn't meant to see. It told of happiness beyond her understanding. And a simple desire to be in bed together now.

Not that they adjourned till they'd filled Becky with apple and blackberry pie, lavished with clotted cream, and cheese and apples and more of that wonderful coffee. It was as if they relished the waiting. But as Becky set off down their drive — "a gentle walk, mind, and no decorating!" — she could hear laughter from the open bedroom window.

★ ★ ★

Tony looked uneasy — or was it simply preoccupied? — when he presented himself at her front door.

"Look," he began, "about this morning."

"But it was a brilliant idea. Look — goodbye King Kong, hello human race!" She moved her head and neck. They were beginning to stiffen up a bit, but Ted had warned her what to do if that happened.

"Yeah — well, we all go to him. But it wasn't that. It was —" At last he stepped in, but stopped. "What the fuck?" He let his mouth hang open.

"I tried to paint the ceiling," she said. "But the moisture in the paint — well, you can see what it did to the paper. I suppose it dissolved the paste."

"I don't know which is best," Tony said, eyeing a sheet which was already halfway off. "To try and fasten that back up or to pull the whole thing down."

She passed him a couple of drawing-pins. "I'll ask George Gaye tomorrow. The trouble is, I can't reach it — you can see one of the steps has broken. And do take care — the others aren't too clever."

Shrugging, he nonetheless tried each one carefully.

"What was Ted saying about your knee?"

The drawing-pins seemed to hold. "There! Oh," he picked his way down again, "he says to watch them. Wear and tear."

"At *your* age! What on earth have you been doing?"

"Cross-country — where were you the other day? I looked for you, like I said."

"I'm sorry. I couldn't resist the chance to get shorn. I'm not so sure about the result, but it's better than it was." She ran her hands through it. She'd have to wash it tonight. Would it ever return to the shape it should be?

"Suits you. Maybe makes your jaw" — he came down the last two steps — "look . . . maybe, just a bit long . . . I — I don't know . . ." He lifted his right hand and ran his fingertips gently down her face. Just as Owen had done.

Just as Owen had done, he held her gaze a moment, then dropped his eyes to her mouth. And then he looked in her eyes again, his own dilated. She froze. Not in panic. No. In anxiety for him.

He meant to kiss her!

It could only be the gentlest of rebuffs. There was little enough tenderness in either of their lives to spurn it ungraciously. As gently as she knew how, she raised her left hand and gently halted his hand's progress, infinitesimally pushing it away. Minutely she shook her head, holding his eyes as unflinchingly as she could. But her smile was meant to show understanding and forgiveness and — yes — a sort of love.

My God, talk about fucking up! Except that was what he wanted to do. He still did. He wanted to fuck with her. Or cry. Most of all cry. She must have held his gaze for ever. And a bit more. Those blue eyes — so soft he wanted to fall into them and drown.

He didn't even know how she'd turned him away from her, and when she'd gone into the kitchen.

He'd better push off now. Before he cocked something else up.

"Tea or coffee?" How did she manage to make her voice as normal as that?

"Nothing."

"Well, the kettle's boiled now. And you were going to tell me what the problem was this morning. Coffee OK?"

Shit. The reason she had her back to him was she was crying. What had he been and gone and done? Half of him wanted to charge in there and — well, let her cry on his shoulder. Except it was his fault she was in tears.

So he sat down. Hell, no wonder she had a bad back if she had to sit on a chair like this. He could kill the OB. Kill him. He'd like to blast his fist into those even-smiling teeth in that pasty fat face and smash every last one. And then work his way down. Bringing Becky here, away from all her friends, giving her a crap job and expecting her to live in a dump like this. The arsehole! He'd probably hinted genteel thoughts of a terribly suitable marriage. Not that he'd ever marry anyone while he could shaft the Daniels creature for free. And others.

She was standing in front of him, holding out a mug of coffee. Wasn't that why he'd started this? To beat the OB to it?

"I still think I'd better go." Now he was sounding like a sulky schoolkid. Humph! That was all he was, really. In her eyes.

She sat down too, not quite opposite him, so they didn't have to eyeball each other.

"So if you weren't at the *Hamlet* rehearsal and you weren't playing rugger, where were you, Tony?"

She did look at him — briefly — but then looked away.

"London. I've got this mate who gave me a lift. There's this geezer that mum knows at LAMDA. And he fixed up an audition. Well, you see I got my A levels last year. They let me take them at some centre — no, not at the school, they wouldn't let me back in lest I pollute the hallowed portals. Oh, I'd been looking after this E for a mate and I got nicked. But the OB managed to fiddle it — Funny Handshake Club maybe. I got a fine, and then it seemed to be part of the deal I came back here."

"But if you go to LAMDA you won't be here."

"I've finished my probation, nearly. And I did tell my probation officer what I was doing — honestly! I'm not that stupid."

"I don't think you're stupid at all, Tony."

She didn't add, "Not even after your cock-up this afternoon".

"When do you go?"

"I don't know. What about Tim — what if I'm not there to look out for him?"

"Can you really imagine his dad letting him go back there?"

"And what — what about you?"

She got to her feet, and walked over to the window. She was biting her lip, as if working something very difficult out.

She turned back to him, but he couldn't see her face because it was backlit. "That's why — that's why I didn't want you to kiss me just then. Because if we'd kissed, if we'd . . . You — I . . . You're the sort of person who'd have felt — well, just what you said. That you ought to stay . . . to protect me. Tony, you mustn't. You must get out, must. Look at me. Trapped all those years. You must be free. You'll make mistakes, sure. But you must make your own mistakes, not try to protect me from the consequences of mine."

Even in the dim light, he could see she was crying. She didn't try to hide the tears, either.

Whatever she'd said, he had to help her. "If Tim goes, if I go — what'll you do? How'll you manage? I mean, I was asking at the Citizens Advice Bureau. If you walk out of this job, you lose this dump. And for all it's a dump, it's well, it's a roof over your head, isn't it? And if you make yourself homeless —"

"It's B&B or a hostel. Quite." She rubbed her face with the heel of her hand.

"What's Owen say?"

"Owen?" she repeated sharply.

"Well, after what you did for Tim. And he did send you those roses."

"He's sent me roses. That's all. He doesn't owe me —"

"Well, I reckon he does. And I shall tell him —"

"You'll do nothing of the sort!"

"OK, OK. Sorry. Keep your hair on. Now you've had it cut, anyway." He risked a grin.

She smiled back. Yes, he was forgiven.

"Does anyone else know about LAMDA?" she asked.

He shook his head. "No. And they mustn't, either. I've sorted accommodation — oh, the parents of this kid at the other school — and everything, and he can't stop me."

"Except he'll have a bloody good try."

"I'm going soon." He stood up and faced her. If her face was in shadow, his would be spotlit by the late afternoon sun.

"You must."

"I'll write. If that's all right."

"You better had. Care of Mrs Gaye. And phone. When I've got a new number."

"I'll try and drop in on the way. But if I can't —" He spread his hands in despair.

She held open her arms, encircling him. He'd no idea how long they stood like that, her rocking him gently just like his mother used to do.

And suddenly he was out in the lane.

And on his own.

CHAPTER
TWENTY-FIVE

Better to have loved and lost than never to have loved at all? Only someone who'd never loved and lost could have said that. Rebecca had lost so much. Tim for a start: she was sure that what she had said to Tony was right — that Owen would find another school for him; Tony — and she had to go round for the next few days looking as carefree as if he'd be at the school for ever; and Owen.

Her heart hurt. And her brain hurt with trying to work out why losing Owen should dim even the other losses.

At first they'd achieved — in a very short time — a pleasant companionship. Two adults with shared interests and a sympathy for each other, at least. Then he'd seemed at least interested in her as a woman. The kisses. The half-promises. The roses. Since then, nothing. And the only factor she could think of to have change things had been his phone conversation with Mrs Gaye. Her warning him to behave himself unless his intentions were honourable.

How did she feel about that? Was it better to be cut off short like this? Or at least to have had some pleasure and then lost it? Half of her said the former. She could get over this. Of course she could. The other produced a sardonic laugh and asked how. No Tim, no Tony to help, either.

Hell, she didn't need help. She'd had fifteen years of unhappiness — yes, a grey, opaque unhappiness, nothing as sharp and vicious as this. And she'd survived. Now Owen had pointed out that her computer literacy was marketable, now she'd shown herself that she could deal with the chaos of the library — now she could see what other jobs there were. She'd find one that really paid. And get her own place — even a room to call her own.

And what would she use for a deposit? No address, no benefit. No address, no job.

All right, then, she'd have to try another tack. She put in operation her plan to search out a solicitor prepared to take on her case on a no-win, no-fee basis. There must be one somewhere. But would she find one in a small town like Newton Abbot, even in Exeter? If only she were eligible for legal aid. Of course, Clifford might well have been lying when he told her that. She must simply get on her bike and find out.

As for getting through today — and the evening celebrations with the teachers — she'd have to act as if for an Oscar.

Perhaps Clifford paid none of his staff very well. Why else should Jeremy Cavendish present himself outside her cottage in a Lada? She'd have expected him to go for something sleek, red and sporty, not boxy, off-white and bumbling. Perhaps they'd achieved cult status over the years since she'd driven Rupert's. Until he'd declared a car too much of an extravagance.

They set off quickly, as if Jeremy were afraid that Clifford might be about to discover him in a sackable subversive act. And certainly they weren't heading for either of the village pubs. What had happened to the courage of these men? Why didn't they make a collective stand against Clifford? Oh, there'd be mortgages, and misguided loyalties. Perhaps some of them were in tied cottages, too. But she'd have thought Reg Sowerby would have made it clear enough to anyone that he drank where and with whom he liked.

Where was the issue at the moment. They'd skirted Newton Abbot and seemed to be heading inland. Place names flashed past in the headlights but meant nothing to her. The roads themselves twisted unceasingly: surely they had major roads in this part of the world? If they did, Jeremy might almost be avoiding them, he turned right or left so often.

He wasn't talking much, and she didn't have much effort left. Not after a day in which Swain had lived up to his nickname, and the scripture teacher had given a tongue-lashing to one of the kids in front of all the library users. She'd intervened, of course — the library was her domain — and made herself unpopular, as if that mattered. And there'd been no Tim, of course, and precious little Tony. He'd appeared briefly at the end of school, and had already leaned confidentially across her table when Swine had surged up. She was positive the message he'd delivered from his father was spurious, but it had deflected Swine.

218

By the end of the fifth mile, Rebecca knew something was very wrong. Grown men wouldn't be so afraid of Clifford that they drank this far from him. Unless it was a special pub, of course. Wasn't it supposed to be manly to go for real ale, which might well be sold at the back of beyond?

"This pub we're going to," she began. "Is it a real ale place or something?"

"Why d'you ask?"

Oh, he *was* in a gracious mood!

"Because," she said, "I'm getting thirsty, and we've passed any number of pubs. So I presume this one is special."

"Yes. That's right. And well away from the Chief's prying eyes."

"Why do you all let him get away with his tyranny?" she asked.

"What on earth d'you mean?"

Wasn't it obvious? "I wouldn't have thought him the easiest of bosses."

"Well, not if you rock the boat like you've been doing. You know, there's always hierarchies in a place like this. You have to work your way up. But you sort of exploded into the place, didn't you?"

"I don't know what you mean. All I did was call an ambulance for Tim. That's hardly explosive."

"There are rules for dealing with things like that. And you never even phoned the school. I mean, don't get me wrong, you did the right thing, and I'm glad young Griffiths is alive to tell the tale. But of course you got up the Chief's nose."

"If that was the price of saving Tim's life, then so be it," she said. She waited for him to agree. "So how much further is it?" she asked a few minutes later.

"Why d'you ask?"

"*Hamlet*'s a curious choice of play for a school this size, isn't it?" she asked, since she couldn't find a polite answer to his question.

"Why?"

"I wouldn't have thought you'd have found sufficient boys either interested or able."

"On the contrary, a captive supply," he retorted.

"That's quantity, not quality."

He paused so long she wondered if he was irritated at being capped by a woman. Or by her, specifically. Still, if he was, that was tough. After fifteen years of biting her tongue for Rupert, she wasn't about to for anyone else. Not now. Not now she'd scented freedom.

"Quite a lot of small parts," he said out of the blue.

"Some quite big ones, too, though. Hamlet, for a start."

"Well, with Tony there's no problem. Between you, me and the gatepost, there's talk that the Chief only brought him back here to play it. I mean, he's got decent A levels. Not good enough for a top university. Or even a good redbrick. But for one of the ex-polytechnics. I don't get the impression he's specially keen on academic success. I'm afraid he'll disappoint his father."

Was he fishing for information? She would pretend she had none to give. "What do you see him doing?"

"Smoking a lot of pot and playing the guitar. Lucky bastard." Cavendish had the grace to chuckle.

At long last they pulled into a car park behind a pub. All around was the sound of wind: wind in trees, wind in heather or broom, perhaps. A high hillside loomed, but she could only guess at the size by the way it blotted the stars, which seemed close enough to touch. No urban light-pollution here, she told herself. This was the place to be with someone with whom you were — in tune. She corrected the thought before it had even emerged. She remembered Tony's excitement, as he dismissed the sea and longed for the moors. And here they must be.

In the distance a horse coughed. And the occasional sheep still baa-ed. All this space. It was so exhilarating. Why, perhaps Cavendish had brought her all this way for a treat! Perhaps his surliness had been a front. Perhaps he had taken such a roundabout route to give everyone else time to get there before her.

She turned to him, laughing. "Oh, isn't this grand! Smell the air up here!"

He laughed too. But was he laughing with or at her? It was impossible to tell.

In itself, the snug was interesting. The inn's walls must have been nearly two feet thick, and the ceiling was low and beamed. There were photos and prints of hunt scenes. A couple of foxes' tails (*brushes*, she corrected herself) over the deep inglenook fireplace, plus some hunting horns. Walls and ceiling had a brownish patina, which might just have owed more to age than to tobacco smoke.

But the snug was empty.

Was a band of middle-aged men hiding somewhere ready to leap out yelling, "Surprise, surprise!"?

She wouldn't hold her breath.

"Well?" she asked.

"Well what?"

"Well, what are we doing out here?"

"Having a quiet drink, aren't we? What's your poison?"

"Is there food?"

"Only in the season," the man behind the bar said. "But there's crisps and nuts and that."

"Mineral water, then, please."

"Only in the season," the man behind the bar said. "But there's soda water, or lemonade."

"Lemonade, then, please." She addressed herself to the barman. She didn't particularly want to speak to Cavendish. But she would have to.

"Oh, come on, have a decent drink," he was saying. "You've come all the way to Devon and I bet you haven't had a drop of cider yet. Come on, they've got a really nice one. Sheep's Clothing, it's called."

"But which of us does it turn into a wolf?" she asked, smiling coolly. "No, not on an empty stomach, thanks."

"Goes to your head, does it?" His smile was suggestive. "Or somewhere else?"

"Oh, definitely somewhere else. My stomach. And I get travel sick. Imagine, in those lanes. I'd hate to mess up your car, Jeremy." She kept her voice light.

They took their drinks over to the far side of the snug, sitting within the inglenook and dodging the occasional spit from the fire. In other company, this would have been fine and romantic. In this company she clearly had to think on her feet. Should she simply ask him outright what had happened to the others? It was a fair question, after all. Or should she ask him directly why he'd lied, why he hadn't asked her out — man to woman?

Or should she simply wait for him to say something?

On the grounds that that might make him feel more uneasy — might give her the ultimate advantage — she would do that. And meanwhile, there was no reason not to enjoy herself.

"Can anyone use the darts?" she asked.

"Sure," he said lazily. "Want me to teach you?"

Did you ever forget how to throw darts? Or was it like riding a bicycle? Well, her legs had still worked after all that cycling, so she would take it as an omen. Rusty her skills might be, but as the erstwhile vice-captain of her own village darts team, neophyte she wasn't.

"Please," she said, allowing her voice to become very little girl.

OK, it was deceitful. But she was rusty and, until she found the weight and balance of the darts, she might just have been an apt learner. At last she got her rhythm, however, and her eye was most certainly in.

"You're doing very well," Cavendish observed. "How about a few bob on the next match?"

Oh, it would be like taking candy from a baby, and much more fun. Especially as a few regulars had turned up and were watching them with interest.

"OK," she said. "Why not? But you should have a handicap!"

The locals nodded in agreement. They might have been a chorus from a Hardy novel. It was only fair, they said, since he'd been teaching the young maid.

Young maid! If only they knew. But the light was dim, her eyes were bright, and she wouldn't correct them. Soon she'd forgotten she was whiling away a lousy evening and started to enjoy herself.

It was so tempting to celebrate with a glass of cider and to leave her stomach to worry about itself. Especially as a party had more or less formed itself around them. But she knew her cider and her stomach of old. And she still had to get back in one piece. The way Cavendish — she still couldn't think of him as Jeremy — was drinking he'd be way over the limit. But not so drunk he wouldn't want to make a detour to a quiet lay-by and try to grope her. The front passenger seat folded flat, backwards, didn't it? A couple of tugs on levers and he could have her flat on her back, vulnerable as a beetle.

No, surely that was stuff for village lads. The sort of lads she'd outwitted when she was a girl. Which made it all the stranger that she'd been sucked in by Rupert, didn't it? Poor old man, he would be rotating in his grave if he could see her enjoying herself like this. And she rather hoped he was.

"It's no good," she said, as they emerged into the Dartmoor night, "I shouldn't have had all that lemonade."

224

"Not going to be sick, are you?" he asked anxiously as he unlocked the driver's door. He got in and reached over the passenger seat to open hers.

"I hope not." She did. She wasn't entirely lying. She got in, suppressing the bubbling in her stomach.

"Can't you take something?"

"Got nothing with me. After all, I wasn't expecting to be driven this far. On straight roads I might be all right. On the sort of thing we came up on — well, I'll try and give you plenty of warning. The trouble is, with the Lada's suspension —"

"Why the fuck didn't you tell me?"

"Because you didn't tell me we were coming to the back of beyond. Just — just take it gently."

There was no doubt he'd had too much. At least on these remote roads, there was very little traffic at this time of night. But he couldn't sustain a good line, and she did begin to feel nauseous — perhaps because she was so afraid.

"I think," she said, "You'd better find somewhere to pull over. Soon."

He did. She didn't somehow think he was the sort of man to hold her forehead at such a moment, which was fine, as she didn't propose to need it held. She disappeared well to the back of the car, waited a few minutes, and then returned — but to the driver's door.

"The only way to stop this happening again," she said truthfully, "is for me to drive. Don't worry — my late husband used to have one of these. I clocked up fifty thousand miles in one."

225

She pulled up with something of a flourish outside the cottage. And got out briskly. Quit while you're winning, she told herself.

He was equally quick. "Aren't you going to invite me in?" he demanded, grabbing her arm. "I mean, you know — well, it was a nice evening."

The funny thing was, it had been. And she'd so enjoyed driving again, even Cavendish's old rattle-trap, with more miles on the clock than Rupert's had when it had been scrapped. There'd been no car after that. A waste of money, he'd said.

"Yes, it was. Thank you for inviting me. Goodnight." Time enough — another, safer time — to ask why he'd invited her to a party that never existed, in a pub in the middle of nowhere.

"What d'you mean, "Goodnight"? Come on, Becky — a bit of gratitude'd be nice. You know, you're supposed to invite me in for coffee."

"If you knew what my place is like, you'd be grateful not to come in. Goodnight, Jeremy."

He grabbed her arm. "Now, come on —"

"Let me go, please. No!"

He was hurting. And he was pushing her backwards up the path.

"Let me go!" she shouted.

"Oh, you'll have to shout louder than that. Get your keys out, woman."

In the bag, not the dowager's bag but the thank-you present from Owen, was Owen's phone. She pretended to burrow for the keys. In fact, her thumb found the touch pad and switched in on. A little green light winked at her. She pressed the bottom right button three times.

"Well?" he said, holding out a hand.

"Well," she said, "I've just dialled 999. And if you don't leave me in peace now, there's no way I'm going to apologise for a false alarm. Get it?"

He got it.

She didn't apologise for a false alarm. She explained to the operator, asking casually, "I suppose there's been no sightings of the peeping Tom tonight?"

They wouldn't tell her, of course. But she locked herself in, and made sure the back door was bolted too. Just for good measure, she wedged chairs against both doors. And she took the phone to bed with her.

CHAPTER
TWENTY-SIX

Rebecca stepped from the gloom of the cottage into a wet, grey world. Sea mist had drifted inland overnight. The drip from the trees was the only sound.

Stiff and sore — the darts had taxed even more muscles than the cycling, she thought — she made the effort to shift the heavy bike out of the outhouse and on to the road. And found she had a flat tyre. No time to sort out a puncture now. And she had to scuttle up that hill very fast if she wasn't to be late.

A couple of staff cars overtook her. Neither was a Lada, however. And neither driver was courteous enough to offer her a lift. In fact the only vehicle that stopped was one coming down, George Gaye's.

"You all right after last night, my dear?"

"Last night?"

"Going out with that young scoundrel! I'm surprised at you, my dear."

"I didn't go out with Cavendish. At least, I did, but that wasn't the intention. He invited me to a staff party. Perhaps none of the others fancied an evening in his company. After last night I can't say I'd blame them."

George still looked concerned. "But you're all right?"

"George: between you and me, I got him drunk, and then drove him home on the basis that I got car-sick. Oh, and I won five pounds from him."

"He's got a nasty reputation. I came round to tell you to call it off only you'd gone."

She peered in the ute cab at him. "There's something else, isn't there, George? Come on, spit it out."

"I don't know. I don't like to upset you."

She waited, head on one side like a bird waiting for a worm. A story about a worm, at least.

"Well, down the Two Lambs, there's this story going round about a young man who's been laying bets about a young woman, see. That he'd take her out and — well, you can guess the rest . . ."

"Make out-of-season hay with her?"

"Hmm. That'd be about it. So you're all right?"

"Tell Mrs Gaye I protected my virtue with lemonade, darts and a mobile phone. I'll drop by and fill in the details as soon as I can. OK? Only now I must fly!"

"How about early this evening, my dear? And then, you and me, we can go along to the darts match at the Two Lambs and see if you're as good as the folk at The Huntsman say you are . . ."

"That's the real Rebecca Hughes and I claim my five pounds!"

Rebecca wheeled round. Against the light, she could only make out a tall slender man framed in the library doorway. He had his arms outstretched and was striding towards her. "Becky! It *is* you!"

"Simon! Simon Bainbridge!" She threw down the date-stamp and ran into his arms. "My God! My God! How did you get here?" She looked up into his handsome, well-groomed face. Oh, age suited him!

"More to the point, Becky, my darling, how did you?" He pushed her gently away from him, and surveyed the place and its inmates. In turn they surveyed him. A frisson swept through the boys suggesting that they recognised him. As well they might. How many hit West End musicals did he have under his narrow, expensive belt? Not that the boys would have known much about those. So what else had he been doing that she didn't know about?

Meanwhile, Swain's nostrils dilated and he rose portentously to his feet. Sowerby raised an eyebrow and shuffled briskly between Swain and Rebecca before stopping, apparently fascinated by something in one of the newspapers.

"I've come to take you to lunch," Simon announced, in that carrying voice of his.

"But it's only ten thirty."

"So? I never said where we were having lunch, did I? It may take a little time to get there." Simon pushed back an elegant jacket sleeve and looked at his watch. "In fact, we may be cutting it a little fine even now. Ms Hughes?" He offered his arm in a gesture Sowerby plainly approved.

By now there was an audience at the library doors. Sowerby beckoned over the smallest of the boys, who scuttled in, never for a moment taking his eyes from Simon. Master and boy exchanged a whisper. A smile flickered across Sowerby's face.

"You know I can't go yet," Rebecca insisted, if unwillingly. "I'm on duty till twelve fifteen. And I have to be back at one fifteen."

"You're going to be very late, then, aren't you? What a shame." He reached for her coat and bag, nodding slightly as he picked them up.

"Simon: I'm working."

"And are they paying? No? Well, it doesn't matter all that much. You're not going to be working here much longer, are you? You're on your way to a job interview."

"Lunch? Job interview? Simon, be serious. You're causing ten kinds of scandal here."

"Only ten? What a bore. I shall have to cause another." He bent and swung her off her feet.

"Put me down!" she hissed. "At least so you can shake hands with Mr Sowerby."

He obliged.

Trying — and completely failing — to keep her face straight, she said, "Mr Sowerby, may I introduce Simon Bainbridge, the composer? Simon, Mr Reg Sowerby, Head of Classics and the last bastion of civilisation here." She clapped her hand over her mouth. What had got into her? Joy, that was what had got into her. An old friend returning to her life after all these years and in such a fashion.

"I believe you have a little local difficulty, my dear," Sowerby said, bowing slightly as he shook hands. "Now, you have such an excellent system in place here that I

231

venture to suggest that I might take your place for the rest of the morning. And I strongly suspect I might prevail on Cavendish to take over this afternoon." He looked at her very shrewdly. "I believe the term is, he owes you one."

Did they have a bush telephone in this part of the world?

"Go and have your lunch, Rebecca. One proviso, Mr Bainbridge." He drew Simon on one side and whispered.

Simon guffawed, and raised a hand as if acknowledging a masterstroke.

Right from the moment they'd tuned their cellos together in the university orchestra, Becky and Simon had been friends. Despite being a postgraduate, with plenty of other demands on his time, he'd made a point of showing her the ropes. He'd even got her a few paid gigs, playing in semi-professional orchestras. Oh, it had been so good to have a friend like him. The moment he'd found out she was studying both music and English, he'd started to nag her — in the kindest, but most insistent way — to write the libretto for the opera he was working on. No dreams of academic success for him, despite being on a Master's course. He wanted to devote his life to writing, not writing about, music. They'd worked on — what was it now? — *Andromache* together. Not, she thought, that it had ever seen the light of day. It had taken itself altogether too seriously. And then Simon had abandoned the operatic for the musical stage. And fame.

232

"Where have you been all these years?" he demanded, letting her into his car. A Porsche. Well, he always had had style.

"Exactly where you left me," she said tartly. "Birmingham."

"So why didn't you write back?"

"I did! I remember the card you sent when I got my degree." She still had it.

"But after then. I wrote and wrote and heard nothing. And then letters came back saying, "Unknown, return to sender"."

She stared at him across the open car door. "I never left."

"That ugly runt of a husband might have sent them back, I suppose?" he said. "Jesus, what the hell did you think you were doing, marrying that little toad?" He went to the driver's side and slid in. "You changed the moment you met him, you know. A sort of Svengali in reverse."

He started the car. It roared into life.

"Where are we going?" she asked.

"Like I said, lunch. Only looking at you I think we'd better have coffee first. And cakes. Where do you suggest? Plymouth? Exeter? Bristol? Or is that too close to Birmingham?"

"Even in this wonderbug it'd take too long to get cakes. Anywhere, Simon, anywhere."

"But you must know somewhere."

"I've only been here a couple of weeks. And I cannot claim that my peregrinations have been extensive."

"Ooh, I love it when you talk dirty. Did Rupert really talk like that? I mean, fancy devoting your life to a bloody book of hard words."

"His life. And mine. And —" She stopped. She mustn't start whinging now. She mustn't waste a moment of her time with him. "Now, I've been to Dawlish — that was in the dark; and Newton Abbot — that was in a hurry; and Exeter — that was in vain, apart from some wellies."

"Trouble is, at this time of year," he said, stopping at the end of the drive to check for traffic, "such a lot of places close down. I think Exeter's the best bet. There may even be some decent shops there, too."

"Tired of Bond Street, are you?" she asked, hoping he wouldn't want to look at her cottage.

"Absolutely," he said. "So did you bump him off? Rupert? God, any man who shares a name with a sartorially challenged bear ought to be bumped off."

"He was run over by a bus. He had this supreme belief that the whole world should stop for him. But when he stepped into the road, this particular bus didn't. The poor driver. It must have been terrible for him. And not his fault at all."

"Was it instant?"

"No. He was in a coma for some days. Oh, Simon, do you know what I used to do? I used to sit watching the bleeps and wonder which machine I could stop so that he died. I so wanted him dead." She reached in her bag for a tissue. "People must have thought I was praying for his recovery. I wasn't. Oh, I wasn't."

234

He reached for her hand and transferred it on to his thigh, where he squeezed it from time to time. "Poor Becky. Poor Becky. But tell me" — she felt the flex of the muscles as he depressed the clutch to change gear and shift the car into real life — "tell me why you never got in touch with me? You know I'd have ridden to the rescue."

Quietly removing her hand, she told him about her life. "I couldn't tell anyone I'd known. The only way to survive was not to look back. Ever. I even gave away my cello — no," she squeaked, as he stared at her and started to drift towards a family car, "it's only a loan, and I've an idea that car likes its wing the shape it is! No, I stopped playing. I closed down all my systems, in a way."

"Like one of those desert flowers that only blooms after rain? Well, sweetheart, today you are going to bloom."

She'd said nothing. It wasn't worth arguing in the car. He wasn't in Mrs Cowley's league when it came to taking risks, but he wasn't the greatest driver in the world. She'd wait till they were having coffee and then tell him. Everything.

He parked in virtually the same spot as Mrs Cowley, even if the Porsche occupied rather more of it than the Mini had. As they sauntered in the direction of the cathedral, she regaled him with tales of Mrs Cowley's derring-do, and her attack on the unwary — and innocent — Owen.

"Which is how you must have got hold of me, isn't it? You must have seen Owen."

"Becky: no one, repeat no one, sees Owen when he's got a panic on. They virtually have to drip feed him. And it's so stupid of him. He's got these lovely commissions and could take his time — you know, they let him hand-pick his own orchestra these days for recording the scores."

She worried a sore spot on her lip. Hardly surprising, was it, that Tim had the chance to take all those photos of the stars, and talked about household names with such ease. And the guy who'd opened the fair — another of his intimates.

"Now, just down here — and, *voilà*! — here's a nice chic little place for a coffee and wonderful cake. Except you should have two. You're far too boney." He sat her down. When was the last time a man had pulled her chair back for her, and eased her into it?

She suppressed a smile. It was hardly surprising two waitresses almost collided with each other in their haste to wait on him. To her he might be dear old Simon, but to these young women he was an extremely handsome man. He'd lost weight too, and the bones of his face held fascinating hollows. Where Owen was fair, Simon was dark almost to the point of swarthy, his hair tumbling and falling as if he were a Byronic hero. There was the tiniest touch of silver at the temples, but that might have been an artistic extra, rather than simply part of the ageing process.

"Now," he said, when they'd ordered, "I hate to say this, Becky, love, but you have reached the age when the human body requires a little assistance from its clothes. And you are getting none. The jacket's OK, but that blouse — whoever told you you could wear beige? It absolutely drains your colour. We'll go and shop for England as soon as we've finished here."

"No, we won't," she said. "I can't, Simon. Last week, I was daft enough to buy some things with my credit card. I've absolutely no hope of paying it off."

"No?"

He didn't even sound bothered.

"I'm — I'm poor, Simon. And if you think — for old times' sake — that you are going to become my Fairy Godfather and transform me, I can't let you. Not unless you can do it with a wand, not money."

"A wand! That's a bit phallic, Becky." He twinkled at her. "Poor, you called yourself. Well, I wouldn't call you poor. Not rich. Not by some people's standards. But certainly not poor. Not with this in your bank account. It should more than cover your credit bills, at least."

He slipped a cheque from his handbag. It sat on the table between them.

"I'm not taking your money," she said, trying not to count the digits in the little box.

"You're not taking my money, Becky. You're taking your money. Remember that tight-arsed little opera I wrote? And your libretto? Well, poor *Andromache* died a death. But one or two of your lyrics didn't. Because we couldn't find you — OK, I should have looked harder! — I had my accountant open a trust fund for you. I put the money in. It grew. Every time anyone, anywhere, played your lyrics, a little more went in."

This time she turned the cheque round and stared.

"You see, they played your lyrics quite a lot. The disc of the show went platinum. And so I used some more of your lyrics in the next. Which also went platinum. Which is where the job interview comes in. Becky: come away with me and write a whole show!"

She'd no idea how long she sat staring, open-mouthed at him. She couldn't have spoken. Ideas were bombarding her far too violently for that. She was rich. By her standards, what was on the cheque in front of her made her rich. No more charity clothes, no more cottage, no more school. But if she went to work with Simon, that meant no more Owen.

But Owen didn't want her: he'd not contacted her because of what Mrs Gaye had said. He wasn't sure. He was backing off. But what if he'd been simply too busy to phone? And he'd certainly taken time out to tell Simon about her.

By now Simon was laughing, showing all those splendid teeth. "My darling Becky! The expression on your face! It isn't very flattering, you know, to have someone gaping at me as if I'd invited her to the scaffold, not a reasonably comfortable island. Let me just settle up, and we'll talk as we walk. The sooner that's in your account the happier I shall be. I had this terrible vision of pulling out the cheque with a flourish only to find it was a tube ticket and I'd chucked away the real thing."

He left an appropriate, not an overwhelming tip, and ushered her out. She could feel the eyes of the women on her, boring into her back, wondering what on earth

238

a mouse like her had done to deserve such a gorgeous man.

He tucked her arm into his. "Now, when I offered you my all, your little hesitation told me everything. You, my beloved Becky, have fallen for our friend Owen, haven't you?"

The blush surged up in her face, throbbing in her cheeks like toothache.

"And you — being you — didn't think you deserved a rich, handsome man in your bed. Not when you were poor and plain. Well, Becky, that hair!"

"You should have seen it before!" she protested, hoping to divert him.

"I heard. All about it. About your clothes. All about them. About your cottage. All about it. From the man himself. At three ten yesterday morning. It seems he'd at last remembered all about me and my interest in you. Well, he'd been working round the clock, poor man, since Saturday. Anyway, he phoned to tell me he'd found you. And told me to keep my lustful paws off you and your lyrics till he'd approached you with a project he had in mind."

Becky stared. Clutching his arm, she shook her head, eyes filling with tears. She'd thought — she'd hoped . . .

"I'd have thought myself they weren't totally incompatible. But he does seem quite unreasonably possessive. Now, sweetie, what we have to do now is go and buy a whole load of black sacks."

She stared. Nothing he was saying made sense. And did it matter? Owen wanted her!

"To put all those charity clothes in, silly. And then we'll go and get some proper clothes to replace them. And then we'll take lunch — I did take the precaution of booking a table at the Ship — and shop a little more before I return you to that outpost of masculinity back there. Right. Lingerie first? Or shoes? Gracious me, I'm not paying. You use your card! Until you reach the limit — then I'll help, you silly girl . . ."

Simon stopped outside the cottage long enough for her to drop off her bags. Then he insisted on running her back up to the school.

"I can't think why you're doing this," she said, standing by the gate. "There's really no need."

"There's every need. I promised that old geezer I'd bring you back safely. There's only one thing." He opened the driver's door, and slid the key into the ignition, but walked round to the passenger door. "Come on. There are the keys. This is the other thing I promised Sowerby. You're driving!"

By now nothing surprised her. She settled in. "Done. Provided I can take it round the block first."

At last she sailed up the drive and parked with a splatter of gravel. "This has been the most magical day."

"I can't help thinking," he said, unfolding himself from the car and coming to help her out, "that you're overdue for a little magic. Now, you will consider my job offer."

"Are you sure it means working in the Western Isles?"

"Where else? Though I do have a little place in Islington."

"Western Isles, no chance. Islington — we'll see." She looked at him under her lashes. "It rather depends on — on Owen's project."

"In that case, I can't envisage seeing all that much of you in Islington — I fancy his will be a pretty exclusive contract. So, until we meet again, farewell."

She went to hug and kiss him, but he was too quick for her, pivoting her on one foot so she lay in his arms back across the Porsche's bonnet.

"Come on, where's your style? Get that leg in the air," he whispered somewhere into her neck. "And feign a snog."

"Are you sure? It won't half damage your street-cred!"

"As if Drew would care!" he muttered, still into her neck.

"You're still with Drew? Oh, Simon, I'm so happy for you!"

And the rest of their words were lost in a huge round of schoolboy applause.

CHAPTER
TWENTY-SEVEN

"Where's he gone? You've been talking to him! Where's he gone?"

Clifford thrust back the front door in Becky's face. He strode in. He meant, no doubt, to slam it behind him. It stuck, still slightly ajar.

She shook her head. "What on earth do you mean, Clifford?" There was only one thing he could mean, wasn't there? But nothing, nothing on this earth would force her to betray Tony's confidence. And to be fair, she'd certainly no idea when he'd gone. She'd rather hoped he'd slip round the previous evening, to congratulate her on her driving and other performances. But when he hadn't appeared, she'd assumed that he couldn't face another emotional episode. And perhaps she'd been relieved to go down to the Gayes and thence to the pub with George. He'd seen her safely home.

"Don't play the innocent with me. I know he's been down here. He was down here on Sunday." Clifford glared at her. She'd never realised how ugly his face was, nor how cruel.

"That's right. He came to see how my bad neck was. After I'd seen the vet."

"And he said nothing?"

"What should he have said?"

He wheeled from her, as if about to search the cottage. His eye lit on the letter she'd been writing. He pounced. "What's this?"

Ah, she'd rather not have had to do this. But she said quietly, "A letter. To you. My notice."

His reaction was worse than she'd feared. Dashing the paper on to the floor, he was across the room in two strides, his hand grabbing her shirt as if she were some boy to fight in the playground. "You. Giving your notice. To me. You!" He pushed her backwards, so she staggered against the wall. "You bitch. You ruin a good man's life. Against my better judgement I take pity on you. I give you work, shelter. And now you — you 'give in your notice'," he mimicked her. "And what do you think you'll do? Without me and my protection."

A damned sight better than with it. But if she said it aloud, it would enrage him further. She said nothing.

"Well? Well? I believe I asked you a question." He towered over her.

Clearly and absolutely, she knew she had to get away from him. He was a big man, heavy. She could outrun him, surely. If she edged to the door and legged it to the village . . .

"Dad! Becky needs you. Now!"

Owen was concentrating so hard on staying awake and steering a straight line he hardly heard. Then the urgency in Tim's voice from the passenger seat registered.

"What the hell — ?"

"Look. Your phone. She's paging you from the other one."

"Answer it. Go on. You know I can hardly use the bloody thing!"

"I've tried. There's no reply. All I get is these noises. Can't you hear?"

Owen listened. He'd thought — if he'd thought anything at all — that Tim was working through the radio stations and had found some drama. "Can you make it any louder?"

The sounds became grunts and thuds.

"Jesus Christ! Look, can you lose her and call the police?"

He could feel Tim staring at him. "Don't just sit there, for God's sake. See what you can do!"

He pushed up the speed still further. But the traffic up Telegraph Hill was heavy, and some stupid sod was trying to prove his manhood by doing fifty in the outside lane. He put the headlights on main beam and started to tailgate him. At last the idiot got the message and pulled over. The Volvo gathered speed purposefully but not quickly enough. If only he had a lighter car with more power.

"It's no good. It seems to be jammed in this mode."

"Can she receive us?"

"I dare say. I say, should you really be doing a hundred and ten?"

"At least if the police pick me up we can get them on the case — just try and talk to her ... And keep trying."

244

He mustn't think of anything. Just the car and the road. He had to get there. He had to keep Tim safe. He had to get there. He had to keep Tim safe. He had . . .

He'd always cursed folk who drove through the village like this. As if nothing mattered but getting there. But nothing did. Not now. Not now he could hear her screaming. What the hell had he been doing, leaving her alone and vulnerable at that cottage when there was that pervert around? Everyone knew men like that graduated to worse and worse crimes. And he'd left her on her own.

The headlights picked up the reflectors of a big car, parked on the wrong side of the road. Fifty yards from her cottage. Once again, Owen flung the car on to the grass and slewed to a halt.

"Stay here and call the police," he said. "I said, stay here."

"Not if someone's hurting Becky."

How much longer could she fight him off? The man was insane. She'd hit him with the Autumn Fair vase, but it hadn't stopped him. She'd tried to fumble the phone from her bag, and had even managed to press the on button, but he'd thrown the whole lot across the room and was bent on getting his hands round her neck. But he didn't want to kill her. Not yet. He'd grabbed her by the hair and was forcing her towards the stairs. God, it was almost funny! He was going to rape her upstairs. Is that what he thought respectable men did, only rape on a bed? But there was only room for one of them on the stairs. If he went first, she'd drag back. If he forced her in front of him, she could kick.

She screamed. She'd screamed herself hoarse, but she'd try again.

Dad would kill him. Not that the bastard didn't deserve it. But he couldn't let his dad do it. Tim grabbed the old-fashioned phone, cursing the time it took the dial to return to zero after each nine. Then — God knew why, but he had to do it — he grabbed his camera and shot from all angles the crazy scene on the stairs. His dad, tall and slight, trying to pull the great fat toad Payne off Becky. All of them facing upstairs. At last Becky broke free, and was trying to run up the stairs and hitch down her skirt and God knows what. And then it was Payne who was yelling — what had Becky done to him? Whatever it was it must have hurt. And then Owen came down fast, with Payne almost on top of him. Now Tim could do something, surely. Drag Payne off his dad. God, he was heavy! Try to hold those flailing arms and legs. And here was Becky beside him, with pairs of tights, for goodness' sake, and she was trying to tie the bastard up. And getting kicked for her pains.

Between them they rolled him on his stomach, and brought his arms behind his back to tie them. If only they could control his legs, kicking with his leather shoes.

And then there was a rush of other feet, and suddenly they didn't have to do anything. The police had arrived.

246

There was so much blood. Not hers. Owen's. His nose was bleeding again. But he was irritably waving the policewoman away. he grabbed a wad of paper towel, but insisted, "It always does this. Just look after Becky. And Tim. My son. He's just getting over concussion."

"That's the young man who called us, is it, Sir?" the policewoman asked. "He seems to have a very cool head, that's all I can say. And getting photos of the incident — very impressive."

Incident! Such a dismissive term for the last half-hour's brutalities. But Becky smiled. She was all right, after all. Bruised — she hurt all over now feeling was coming back. And very shaken. But triumphant. No, the brute hadn't raped her. But it had been a close-run thing. And only now was her brain coming back into gear.

"How did you get here?" she asked Owen, passing more kitchen towel.

"Thanks. Tony rang us. Said he'd skipped. Said you shouldn't be left to his father's anger. So we came up."

"But the music —"

"Finished it at three this afternoon. But when Tony rang — well, I've never seen Tim move so fast. He packed the car. Everything was ready by the time the courier had collected the score. We came as quickly as we could. And, then, when I saw him — saw you — I thought —"

"He didn't rape me." Becky looked at each face in turn. Owen's, Tim's, the policewoman's. "He didn't rape me. Though I admit he had a damned good try. Can I go and change? I feel — soiled."

"We'd rather you waited till you get to the station," the policewoman said. "There may be — evidence — on your clothes. But I'll go and pack a bag for you."

"Make it an overnight bag," Owen said. "She won't be coming back here."

"Where are your things, then, Rebecca?" the policewoman asked.

Becky started to laugh. "Not upstairs. Not upstairs! In the outhouse."

The officer looked blank. "The outhouse?"

"Haven't you noticed the smell in here? The damp? Well, I bought some new clothes yesterday, and I didn't want them to smell. But — oh, dear — there's such a lot and —"

"Can you sort out what she'll need for tonight? And — would you mind putting everything else in my car? I didn't lock it."

"I'll give her a hand, shall I?" Tim slid after her.

Alone in the kitchen, they stared at each other. She could feel his eyes taking in every bruise, every scratch. All she could see was his exhausted face, pale, haggard. Then she heard him say, "That's OK, isn't it? You will come back with me?"

"Try stopping me," she said.

CHAPTER
TWENTY-EIGHT

How she could ever have imagined missing Owen's fireworks display? The sky was alight with every colour a child could imagine. Nearer the ground the field swirled with gunpowder smoke, the smell blending with baking potatoes, punch, and the barbecue.

"All that money going up in flames," Tamsin was saying. "He might as well be burning five pound notes, just to show us how much he's got. Now, Jack — you be careful with that sparkler . . ."

Becky heard but passed on without commenting. There were the Gayes, both ready with a hug and a kind word. And over there she saw Simon, with Drew, short and fat and no one's idea of a lifetime's partner, yet as adored by Simon as in their first year together. So where was Owen?

Tim was deep in conversation with a pretty girl with a skirt barely covering her bottom, despite the chill of the night. No need to worry about him. No need to worry about Tony, safe in London — but burdened with the knowledge that his father was a criminal.

Where was Owen?

All these faces, familiar but not familiar. Owen's friends, the ones she'd been afraid to face. Most had

249

looked at her curiously — this woman with two black eyes and scabs on her face. But they'd obviously been briefed by Owen or the grapevine, and Becky felt warm under their kindness.

Where was Owen?

On impulse, she turned back towards the house. And there he was, running towards her, and now she to him, as if they were a couple of kids.

They'd both been tense, restrained, after the assault. He'd brought her back to his house after their hours at the police station, exhausted as she but still kind, still solicitous.

"This is your room," he'd said, opening the door and switching on the light. Charming, elegant. But not his.

He'd seemed to be trying to remember a speech he'd prepared — he'd had long enough to work on it all those hours she'd spent making her statement. Perhaps — believing she'd been raped — he no longer wanted anything to do with her. No. She didn't believe that of him. But she — did she want a man at that moment?

At last they'd given up on words, and somehow they'd found each other's arms. They'd still been together, wrapped tight as children, when they'd woken twelve hours later. He'd had to peel her clothes from her, layer by layer, with nothing more romantic to massage her with than witch hazel. And once or twice his tears.

Tenderness, comfort — but, until the bruises and the cuts began to heal, no passion. Not yet. She looked at him now — the bones of his face, his eyes, his lips — and felt every last pain melt away in one rush of desire.

250

She reached up to him. There. She kissed him full on the lips. He couldn't doubt that.

"Do you suppose anyone needs us, just at the moment?" he asked, trying to sound casual, his eyes giving him away.

"I think that waiter would like us to relieve him of that bottle of champagne," she suggested. "And maybe a couple of glasses." Her face too was straight, but her eyes were holding, challenging his.

"But other people might want to share it with us."

"They wouldn't know we'd got it if we took it indoors."

"If we took it indoors we might not get any of that roast pork."

"I'm quite fond of that pig: it would be like eating an old friend."

"And we might not be able to see the fireworks."

"I think," she said, "it's time to make a few fireworks of our own. Don't you?"

For answer he took her hand and led her back to the house.

ISIS publish a wide range of books in large print, from fiction to biography. Any suggestions for books you would like to see in large print or audio are always welcome. Please send to the Editorial department at:

ISIS Publishing Ltd.
7 Centremead
Osney Mead
Oxford OX2 0ES
(01865) 250 333

A full list of titles is available free of charge from:
Ulverscroft large print books

(UK)
The Green
Bradgate Road, Anstey
Leicester LE7 7FU
Tel: (0116) 236 4325

(Australia)
P.O Box 953
Crows Nest
NSW 1585
Tel: (02) 9436 2622

(USA)
1881 Ridge Road
P.O Box 1230, West Seneca,
N.Y. 14224-1230
Tel: (716) 674 4270

(Canada)
P.O Box 80038
Burlington
Ontario L7L 6B1
Tel: (905) 637 8734

(New Zealand)
P.O Box 456
Feilding
Tel: (06) 323 6828

Details of **ISIS** complete and unabridged audio books are also available from these offices. Alternatively, contact your local library for details of their collection of **ISIS** large print and unabridged audio books.